MEDUSA

Also by John Fraser
and published by AESOP Modern Fiction:

Animal Tales
Black Masks
Blue Light / Starting Over
The Case
Down from the Stars
Enterprising Women
Hard Places
An Illusion of Sun
The Magnificent Wurlitzer
Military Roads
The Observatory
The Other Shore
The Red Tank
Runners
Soft Landing
The Storm
Three Beauties
Wayfaring

MEDUSA

John Fraser

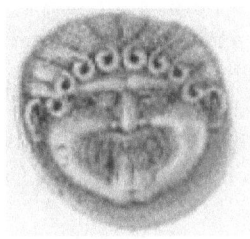

AESOP Modern Fiction
Oxford

AESOP Modern Fiction
An imprint of AESOP Publications
Martin Noble Editorial / AESOP
28 Abberbury Road, Oxford OX4 4ES, UK
www.aesopbooks.com

www.johnfraser.info

A catalogue record of this book is
available from the British Library.

ISBN: 978-0-9927588-9-9

Contents

Foreword		**7**
Medusa I		**9**
1	Disaster	**11**
2	The Moving Wall	**19**
3	Franco, a Dealer	**29**
4	Bella	**41**
5	Dr Hani	**63**
6	Travelling	**89**
Medusa II		**97**
7	Home	**99**
8	Escorting	**129**
9	Exploring	**141**
10	Smara	**173**
11	China	**191**
Coda		**201**

*'And may pure reason rather than experience
persuade, that the universe can collapse,
borne down with a frightful-sounding crash.'*

Lucretius, De rerum natura, V.

*'Cette chose nous l'avons voulue. Nous l'accomplissons. Nous
marchons vers le but armés de tous ces jours d'attente, de tous ce
qui fermenta en nous depuis notre naissance.
Aujourd'hui, joie: elle s'épanouit, elle fleurit sous mes pas ...'*

Smara. Carnets de voyage de Michel Vieuchange.
Publiés par Jean Vieuchange. Plon. Paris, 1932.

Foreword

MEDUSA was one of the three Gorgon sisters, the only mortal one, whose looks turned people to stone. She was seduced by Neptune the sea god, in the temple of Minerva, goddess of war. Later, Perseus decapitated her, and put her head on the shield of Minerva, which he had borrowed. Blood from the head, now covered with snakes, dripped to produce the snakes of Africa. It retained its power to turn the onlooker to stone.

Medusa was the name of the French ship, whose wreck was celebrated in the famous, scandalous picture by Géricault, as the raft, bearing crew members and passengers, was left by the officers to drift for thirteen days while they fled in the ship's boats.

MEDUSA I

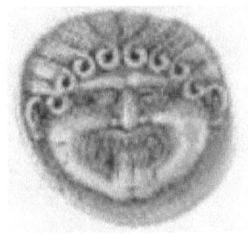

1   Disaster

S O, EVIL strikes again, I say, and laugh.

People, a beautiful carpet, cover this terra cotta plain.

The headcloths, tribalised. Fine liveried goats in black and brown and white. A touch of heavenly blue – that's plastic – all now composed and just a-buzz, still as a carpet from Shiraz that barely stirs with little animals and runes.

Don't let the secret out.

Uselessly, I ask my friend – friend I should bring to justice, or more likely, shove justice in his face, 'What was this – catastrophe? Earthquake again? Or politics? Identity wars? Or grazing grounds? Or just because it's goddam hot,' that brings this press of people here, shucked from their homes and business. And so I think of drinks, cool bars.

Now, we shall start to pack these guys and gals

– here, some are dying, some will soon, and some will wish they were – squared off in tents. Neat.

History will start all over; these will become the hunters, gatherers, and we the fractious gods like Jupiters, assuaging our desires and few of theirs – with showers of coins or flights of swans. Then, let us unpack our boxes – our trove of things incongruous. That's civilisation. Speeded up and started over. Warriors first, then farmers, later – lawyers. Catastrophe and after – and we are the guys who patch it over, tweak the mechanism – off they go again. Everybody!

We fix disasters.

Let's suppose – the airship, squats down on the river, an immense donut. Tiny bodies falling from the sides, as finally, with foam and fire, it hits the grey-green water. Cars stop to watch – the thing should float, must have been planned like that, but no, it sinks, small citizens are drowning in their private drama. Here's a tired helicopter bringing journalists, some leap in with cameras and such.

It's so quiet, so peaceful.

Now, I've nothing better to do. Back in town, I ask the trainman, 'What line is this? I shouldn't have come with you.'

'Eighty', he says, behind the partition where he's received his guests, ingratiating – 'Ah, Geometer this, Engineer that.'

The train is nearly dark. 'Stops by request', we stop in Two Horses for an age, then jump and blur the Caustic Marches, Pyres.

'I'll just retrace my steps,' I say. 'Later I'll make this trip.'

I leave him, ask a woman as she goes home, 'Did a girl, maybe she's in crisis, looking for work, disappear in there where you both live?'

'We're all called women now, not girls. Why do you care? Some kind of molestation? Morbid tricks?'

'Time on my hands. In this place, if you don't speak the language well, the cops will pick you up for loitering, you have to say in dialect, "Fuck off, and on your pony, guy," and then you're safe.'

She says, 'We've all got crises here.'

I give her my friend's name: 'He's done some beastly things. A dance of death.'

She wore her crisis like a shawl. 'You'll have to wait,' she says.

'Absolutely not – I have to find my friends, and then this girl, this woman . . .'

'Maybe their house has been demolished. Or rebuilt. Elsewhere.'

'It all seems a bit secret.'

Why don't I take the 80 back, and start again? It's all portentous, comes from only living once – I'll ask the trainman, but don't want to leave, I'm in this bar beneath the block where that girl disappeared, the district dull, deserted now but surely populous, the guys all doing who knows what, their ladies cooking, maybe on the phone . . . My documents are with my friend, the numbers, all the stuff you need to navigate, find where you are.

'Don't wait for me,' the girl had said, no other choice, but now the bar is closing, maybe a funeral that's passing, maybe the current's off, no games or neon, coffee on the blink . . . And what the fuck's her name? Try pushing all the bells, each one with two, three, surnames, – here starts harassment or abuse, so stop. Locked out and at a loss. At once you're just a stack of bones with dodgy flesh, exams all fudged or bought, your life a stack of Martian whispers.

Trouble, and cop asks, 'Who are you?'

Dammit, I know; I wish I didn't, wasn't here, some murder, suicide or other mystery. 'Oh no, I didn't know her,' into the slammer with him, no documents, prevaricator, molester even, don't know fuck about him! Nice feeling, found out and shameless; scary too, the devil made me see the world – a precious experience – but in the end, Satan is not behind me – stands there, in a cone of light.

Down the devilman!

Well, all is resolved, and here's my friend, the woman's traced as well, will pass into history soon. I tell him, 'I'm tired of all this humanitarian stuff.' Smoke from fires of sticks comes faintly to us, like a morning-after smell of ciggies in cheap hotels.

'Tired of cutting deals with monsters from the battlefields,' I say, 'buying, selling packs of dead and wounded, our dead souls . . . tired of guys disposing, going on TV, morality and ethics – "these guys we kill and those we save", "this dam we build and that we breach". At least the monsters have a grievance, or a need – and they are being hunted. Then, there's all the religious crap . . .'

My friend now waggles his turbaned head, disclaiming routes to God's intelligence. 'Don't blame me,' he says. 'I just protect my guys, I didn't start all this.'

He goes on, 'You're so gloomy.'

'No, not at all. It's always been much worse.'

'Well, that should cheer you up – it's just some guys go down, we pick them up, is all,'

'That's it,' I say. 'And there's no hell, it's been

retired. Maybe heaven too . . .'

He says, 'You need to ask the pope, he specialises. Progressive creeds like ours – they don't have all these fables . . .'

'Go to the root.'

'Exactly. Besides, in democracies some things aren't even asked. Do you prefer pants or gowns? These things just come about, pedalling your bike in gowns is tough, besides, pants is cheaper, don't make you look an idiot.'

'I see how this extends to lots of things. Don't ask. Good or bad, applied to people.'

'Too right. Of course, we'd all vote to be rich and powerful – but that's the one thing you can't do, it seems. You just hold back, and wait.' And he goes on, 'Though someone's got to have them, big bucks and such – you just enjoy and shop a little, have someone to do the work at home.'

Chew some coca. Helps running up and down the peaks – helps also on the plains, and in your car – it's an identity, so fuck you if the culture isn't yours.

We talk some more about catastrophe, the

climate stuff, and how we seem to kill the friend beneath our feet.

'This earth, air, water, fire,' I say, 'this stuff, this nature. Friend or foe, indifferent, now it kills us, maybe it's our fault? I'm not equipped to handle it. I deal with people, proximately – how do I know how many types of frogs it takes to make us happy?'

'Frogs is quite low down, they say.'

'So's some humans, but I can't say that.'

'But you do,' he says.

'Let people take it as a kind of threat. You can't threaten frogs, though.'

He says, 'You can't make people form fours and tell them that they're free.'

'Stalemate forever, then. Or patching, creatively,' I say. 'I expect they had to patch the ark – inventing new techniques ...'

'And yet the fish were quite at home. There's a design – at least for fish.'

2   The Moving Wall

ESIGN's the thing.

Artificial city. Green estranged from nature, cars scuttling, walkers mostly lovers, or running so as to live for ever – buildings ochre, tilting gyroscopes to show you top and sides. No one looks out, nor leaps. Helicopters peering in to land, mosquito-like, on roofs. No cop cars, though there is an ambulance.

Artificial city on a screen, a moving wall – people idle in to this arcade, to watch this fake, dream of a generation past or yet to come. Paradise or curio – depends on where you're from.

Real city – no longer making kettles, caftans or edicts – though lots of prostitutes, and people with nothing much to do, on visits or just picking rubbish – depends on where you're from. The vast periphery, earth hacked out, the trees deleted – for some, a dream, and others – watchful horror.

Dull, that screen city, bughouse with idle bugs. You go outside – real city: there's breaking news and fresh deliveries, even your own rebirth. There's promise – not to raise you up, but maybe jiggle up a step or two. Perhaps your token hits three fruits – then you're a star, and rich with all the tokens you can lift. The others are so gullible.

That automaton – who devised it? Set its wheels a-spinning, shoppers all a-shopping? What happens to those little cars and pickups when they reach screen's edge – pass on to landfill, or re-emerge like movie actors, back at a new, nearly identical, beginning?

Who rules Real City? Both cities, real and spoof, have a history whited out, of origins, both confidently truck towards a sure future. Sure, though no one knows it. Those broad boulevards, the *chaussées* – built like post-Comune Paris. Is revolution expected here, prevented? Or is real city built for traffic, not for politics? Good fields of fire for weapons, carried in sports bags, fired in the name of God, some strong man, pure Idea with ten minutes left to live and aim. Self-slaying concentration, down goes modernity, over flat sights comes purity and its party.

'Could we put that on the screen?'

'No, it's just video games.'

All that mystery, someone's design.

Hector, once warrior, now a Boss.

There must be justice somewhere – my friend's a guilty person, and I need some help in punishing – so go to a professional.

He's a boss. You can tell. Hector, practised in the use of arms.

He lays his green cigar on the veneer. It spits and crackles.

'Natural saltpetre,' he says, 'and an unhappy plant.'

No comment is possible. The smoke has an edge of urine. Maybe rolled too high up on the thigh. He peers at me intensely. 'You know, I'm a convert.'

'Really? To what?'

'I'm being instructed in a number of ...' he pauses, searches, 'Paths to holiness. Monotheism first. Then on to animals and gurus.'

'Don't you have to choose and exclude?'

'Who gives a fuck for what the rules say? It's serious stuff, this quest to be a holy man. You must have seen a few.'

I say, 'After a few years in camps, you find the sanctity evaporates. Mine too.'

'Well, you want favours, better ask them now. When I've graduated, you know, all life is sacred, you can't snuff your friends,' and he laughs and pulls on his smoke as if it's a bottle. His chest rises, deflates, and his belly drops sharply down, his pants seem full of disparate things and voids, his shoes are lizard – maybe those big iguanas. Flesh tastes like chicken.

He mocks me and my job:

'This guy comes to me, he moans a little about how hard it is! – sitting somewhere, some office –

he orders helicopters. "Oh the humanity," and, I suppose, now he wants that I eliminate someone. What a life he has! Goddam harder being refugees and suchlike . . .! and he stares, my pants and shoes, cigar like it's a serpent. And I'm the bad guy that he gives the chance to – for redemption. With a little shooter I'm supposed to give him. Maybe he sets me on some bike, I'm jingling about behind, and I'm about to shoot some guy – his friend – I've never seen before, and if it all goes wrong, the fault is mine, he says, "You stupid criminal! Who cares how long they send you down, or maybe kill you, so's your face falls in your dinner and how great you'll look in colour for the millions."

'I tell him, since he doesn't comprehend my quest for holiness, "Kill your own friend, my friend!" You think, because I walk the line that sorts out good from bad, my life's just territory, and competition, a business plan that says: "Here's stuff to smoke" or maybe zombies, set to work, from some sad place your average guy can't point to, or just slapping gals around . . . And so, he thinks, who'd care, if this one – me – or any other boss gets zapped?

'Well, I'd care, thank you, if it's me.'

He goes on, to himself he's infinitely interesting:

'I've read the books, collected parchments, waltzed the first round with some moo-face the President's picked up – but I don't boast! I saw the politics come down, unravelling – the communist guys just didn't see that people love to buy stuff, don't care how or why it comes.

'Or else they want to find some guy, in Lanzhou maybe, they can play electric draughts with.

'It's goals, it's discipline that matters, but that's all beyond them, that's why politicos must tax them and read their diaries – if you want to make your average guy a noble animal, that's what you have to do. Forced to be free. I saw it all come down, and now the top guys steal, that's fine – but leave a dreg or two! Just take the cash – but just enough it looks like the vault's still full, and give the guys some bucks to make them laugh – they work like fuck, but they're just stupid guys who don't know much. So, give them cash so they can spend some more – they're magic chickens: when you pluck them, out spring bigger feathers, over start again . . . Now, you, this guy, look sad. You think I'll put my holiness on hold, I'll do some dirty job for you and take your gold . . .' and so and so.

The boss's room is long and low. He points, and on the far wall there is a screen, a fresco, oriental maybe, white jade or water, touch of *anis*, *mistrà*, receding, those usual fish or butterflies that rise and fall. He points to them, and asks, 'Why are they there? Drawing our sight into, towards – what – their game?'

Strange things, from a boss, even a little boss.

He says, 'When you follow Mind, design of someone you don't know and wouldn't want to, even dislike as foreign to you – still you know it's Mind you're after. Yours, his or hers – there is no sum, no one plus one, no wrestling for a meaning. Just minds that play at being Mind.'

'I suppose so. No, I don't grasp it. I don't grasp that it matters.'

He sniffs, 'Well, what did you expect – a boss that's sitting here and ordering about a bunch of scum that hovers round and has to kill some unknown guy for unknown what, with me, just sitting still, my eyes fixed briefly on what the dead will contemplate for ever?'

I say, 'I remember the quote from somewhere.'
He waits, he nods.

Shit. He's not going to help me.

Sit in the park. Some guys are throwing sharp killer discs at trees; pet birds, escaped, are in the leaves – copper-orange, mosque blue, soft eyes. It's turning into wilderness, starting over – here too, there are tents, and mud, a plastic jug, a little fire. I am the kindly one, and we'll keep safe the guys that camp out here. Derelicts, hulks they're called, like sinking ships.

I sit and sit, cold eye. Someone's responsible, and must pay – for something. Vendetta. Justice – even, specially, to your friends. You wanted the angel of death – well, you got it, me!

The news is that everything's a plot – once paranoia, now, it's true! The game is speeding up – the end is nigh, and calculated – one year soon there'll be no calendars. Fix the disaster – whoops, here comes another, down go the mountains, nature gives a screech – she's dead! It's no one's fault, but guilt is universal, I and my friend, we race to be the one that's slid away, down the polished slide we go! Escape!

The empires fail, and new ones rise and – phut! they're gone, no time to coin the fables and the rites. No takers for the ark – who'd trust a wooden ship on acid seas?

Only the sun, invincible companion, still trucks up and down the sky and round and round – reminds us of those honey days we never had. It's heavy stuff.

The sun will eat us up. I'm pissed, and when

you're drunk, you tell a bit more, bit less, than the truth. Time to laugh.

    I try again.

3   Franco, a Dealer

THIS GUY is selling, and I say, 'I want a revolver. Those little brass shell-diddies that spew out – all too fiddly.'

He brings out a long shooter, like we had when we were nine.

He says, 'You need a horse to go with this. Just – never near your face, you'll lose an eye. So, wear a wetsuit, shave your head, nose, eyebrows too. Don't speak, don't sneeze.'

'That powder stuff – it makes you sneeze.'

'What currencies you carry?' he asks.

I tell, he makes an angry trip, around the Grand Canyon, Wall of China – he slams my moneys:

'Those guys can't make a die,' he says. 'Now, when the Arabs were on top, they told it right, "This here's a good round lump of junk, and this is me, my overlord is hum, my father's hohum, whoever he might be, my spiritual chief is hokum pokum far away – and here's a picture, lion or eagle, even my new house, whatever takes my fancy . . ." Who makes coins now? Put on them what they like – "I'm little chief, big chief is that, what I believe in is this book, this phantom, eggplant or Mercedes, what you will . . ." No, no one does it now, the truth. How you gonna pay?'

'I've got this ingot, triple nines.'

'Hah, I saw the bulge, thought you were carrying. You know, a shooter drags you down and spoils your line. I've an old raincoat you could have, the pocket's hollowed out. A holster for your gun.'

'How much the lot?'

A figure.

'That's twice as much as we'd agreed.'

'That was on the phone, and seeing you I thought that you was carrying. I'll microwave a shaving from your slab.'

He pours a helping in a ladle, waiting till it cools, and blows some powder off the scales. We sneeze.

'I still don't see why the price went up,' I say.

'I thought you came in armed, to buy another piece.'

If that's the tune, then I must dance – I skitter out, the raincoat wagging with its weight. I hear him shout, 'Try it out on someone first, before . . .'

I'm quite affable all day.

That evening, there's a cop in my room. Formal, he says, 'I'm not a cop, I'm a detective.'

'Excuse me.'

'You been buying shooters.'

'It's in my wittgenstein.'

'Which is what?'

'I hollowed out the Investigations. The muzzle's sticking out.'

'No denial, then?' he asks.

'I find that part demeaning.'

The guy looks like a banker, though his trainers are a fake, the face seen better days and not enjoyed them, tie without colours, and I say, 'The gunseller must be close to you?'

He says, 'You humanitarians piss me off.'

'I'm in the job of sorting out,' I say. 'Quick from the dead, live from condemned. People that can start from scratch, and those that won't. In the end, who knows, some justice.'

'Well,' he says, 'seeing as you're quite a tall poppy, let's say it was for protection, then we'll spy on you.'

So we parley on, he says, and grins, 'Doing you some multiple good turns. Next time we'll talk a deal.'

'My money?' I say. 'Credibility?'

'Are gone, spent, I'm afraid. Being a criminal's not an easy thing. Your heart must plunge right in.'

We cosy down.

'You're a real gent,' he says.

'Don't persist – for me, gents is just a name on a door.'

He pretends to be hurt. 'It's just opinion.'

'I've enough of them myself. Don't want yours too.'

A little silence, then: 'So, this other guy, humanitarian, your friend. You want to bring him justice, with a gun?'

'Justice that you do yourself is called another thing,' I say. 'I couldn't find a guy to help me, so – it's up to me.'

'Because he killed a lot of guys? You all do that, but by omission. Nothing wrong in that.'

'Too late for silly tears,' I say. 'Repentance never comes. Forgetting, pardon, always in the wings. Something harsh is needed. Another cadaver joins the pile – this time with eyes cut open. It's common knowledge – human project's finished, no one's to blame.'

Planet, that old man o'war, is sinking, what does it all mean, I ask, – the latest alibi, humanism with wings – it's all too late. Before we all go down – some little justice, close to home. Right now – it's for my friend! Justice!

I remember –

Old men in white, sleeping on their cleft sticks. Their flocks are gone, stolen or driven off, gunned down for fun or idleness. Dead goats, snuffed out to right some wrong. One of our favourite animals, their yellow eyes in psalters and in bowers, we love their cloven hooves, they're part of us, we hug them close, we wear their horns – to butt with, or as cuckolds. Now, all driven off. The old men sleep, their sheets wound tight to keep the body whole – a white so startling, it's like a hole in the canvas, picture confected just like life, but in those human shapes in white it seems you see the something – nothing – that's beyond, behind.

I asked my friend, 'Why, how, do they sleep on sticks?'

'To be alert, not to lie down, be supine. How the fuck should I know, never tried it.'

'You think we'll have to let them go?' I say, 'Death?'

'They'll all die soon. Just hustle it along.'

'But they carry all the culture, all the songs, the poetry. What'll the kids have to put into their heads?'

'This culture stuff – it's not like you,' he says. 'The kids grow up like us. Quite soon, they find that there's enough complicated things for everyone. We have to let the weak die, to give the weak a chance to live.'

'It's not quite right,' I say.

I don't know why. It's the necessity. We stand together, the two generals, a pact before the battle – our beautiful guards, their horses, all those widows, lovers, right now muddied up and blown away. A pact, a quiet retreat. Don't talk to me of revolution, turn away, turn all those fucking soldiers into something else. What? Don't know.

I call the cop. 'My ingot?'

'Ah yes, that waterproof,' he says. 'We furnaced it, and by the way, I'm a detective, not a cop.'

I curse him, ask the dealer – Franco – for what's left – 'And by the way, you didn't have to smelt the gold, just cut and weigh.'

He laughs, and in the safe there's stacks of tiny ingots, labelled with his name, stamped with three nines.

He says, 'Now we've resolved all that, you know I saved you from one horn of your dilemma. Murder isn't justified by murder,' primly.

'This guy, my friend,' I say, 'let's call him Mr Nemo – here in the earthquake there's a bunch of guys and gals beneath some slabs. Some sing, some pray, our crew is standing round, eyes all a-stare with inner life, and not much going into them. And Nemo says, "Come on, we can't do nothing here," for nothing shifts, and so he finds a tractor, down a last wall, and buries all the singers, safe and dumb.'

The dealer says, 'Rough justice, yes, but justice for the greater good.'

'Then, in another place, some guys are rocketing, so we are stuck. Finds this long gun that's hidden here and loaded, and he pulls the lanyard – noise is like a blow. It seems he hit some structure – no more rockets, no more songs or prayers from whomsoever.'

'Well, there's accusations,' the dealer says, 'here's your two, a third is surely due . . .'

'He gets a gang of our guys, kits them up with arms and such, they go and kill another bunch of guys, the prayers and chants have tired us out. Now, surely that has breached some limit – though all's done in name of liberation, all that stuff . . . salvation.'

The dealer, Franco, says, 'Well, there's the third, a clincher that's quite biblical – though I guess you have no faith yourself, or very little?'

'Nemo's not poor or stupid. I think he earns extinction as – a traitor to our cause, although to save humanity by working at extremes – the endgame, if you follow me – we run, and take, some risks ...'

He says, 'Well, I guess, if you really want, saving humanity, this guy is off the scale, but then, haha, that's quite the point – he's an extreme. Go save him.'

I feel that's not the point at all, the power of words just fails me, and I shout, 'You're just a thief.'

'And you can't aim the necessary bullet!' he shouts.

So, as he screams at me, I skitter out a second time.

Wander up and down, and here's a concert – I go in. They call it 'Mouths and Forks'. There is a screen, the mouths squelch emptily in silence. I hear the broken harmonies – of eating forks, of tuning forks, and then of digging forks and caves, I'm drawn into these openings, the pink and warm red, the dank and depth of black. Nearly giggling, I think of pitchforks; the music whirrs, it slavers round the hall, I think 'San Petronio', the brass choirs, notes tongued and lipped, saliva tipped, the space huge belly, not a mouth – ingestion, digestion – and excretion somewhere. Religion included, and a text – and now it's cantilena, spaghetti sucked in, waggling – despair, down everlasting, down and not reborn.

That was fun. Drives famine out your mind – the sound is horrid, but, as they say, 'it all makes broth', you have to eat, to get it down. It's duty in a way, and quite essential.

4 Bella

ERE'S the girl I couldn't find. The new one. I say, 'They couldn't tell me, and I'd lost my papers. But we had a kind of date.' She's silent. Bella.

I say, 'You could get those teeth fixed. You know what they say – the million dollar smile. Doesn't seem a great sum now.'

'That doesn't seem appropriate,' she says.

'The perfect mouth, the perfect word. Put us all at ease, not watching your snaggle,' though otherwise she's quite OK.

'It might get more from sponsors . . .' uncertainly she says.

'And all the bad guys we do deals with.'

Oh the tedium. Oh the human, all too human. Stuck on this raft, this raft of the *Medusa* – ship is sinking bravely – and we're adrift, the sun will eat us up, so what the hell, why bother, calendar's worked out, it all will end. Raft – at the mercy of each other, who's to eat and who's to dump, and who's to get a ration. Landfall on some hot rock and getting hotter. 'Who's to be saved?' I say aloud.

She says, boldly, 'Too much realism spoils the picture.'

'It doesn't matter,' I say. 'Just – onward, till they eat you.'

She's a pedant: 'Think of everyone as onions – layers on layer – peoples, languages, and wars and sacrifices, life in the galleys, on the shore and on the street and in the garbage, riding on elephants and stealing them. All on all, nothing on nothing, all the ghosts gone down like eaten animals, the earth is made of bones but never poking through.'

She has a fine tongue. And goes on, 'Grudges eliminated, brutalities are cancelled out by those done in our name, all guilty, we've done nothing, there's no sin, but all's forgiven, sin is everywhere reborn. History is awful, but has made us clean. We're all onions but we start today unlayered, odourless and tasteless. White onions, with black-brown-red and yellow skins.'

'OK, you get the job. You're a miracle.'

'You mustn't say that.'

'May I say something?' I ask.

'Couldn't care less,' she says. 'You people who work with people – for people, as you say – you all have something of the corpse. Like old books. Saying and thinking too much. I guess you do care,' and she laughs.

'You say it nicely. Saying and thinking get in the way.'

She presses on, 'It's just there's nothing new in there, it's the old litany, same old boneyard. Tinker and patch.'

'You're right,' I say.

'It's just service.'

'*Objets trouvés.*'

She looks at me like I'm dead meat.

I tell her, 'There are some things I could say.'

She's incurious, 'Such as?'

'I could peel off your hot sticky clothes.'

She turns this up and down. 'You see? The

same old stuff. Quite primordial.'

She's denounced me. Here's the committee. My indefensible behaviour.

They ask, 'Cosmetic dentistry for the workers?'

'Straight teeth mean straight talking.'

'None of your business. Organise, and if there's something left, you show compassion.'

I try to tell them, 'These guys we deal with now – they're guilty victims. Got driven out because they lost their cause.'

'None of your business.'

'Talking of compassion,' I say, 'shouldn't there be an even bigger boss, to ladle in the values?'

The chair says, 'Ultimately, we have religious roots.'

'You want the voice of God – I'm just his finger, lining things up and digging pits.'

'After all, they're victims.'

I say, 'You today, me tomorrow.'

'Exactly.'

Maybe I've no response, maybe I just want to be thrown out.

'No answer, if you don't have the question,' I say. 'Let's just straighten the teeth business before we go to altruism and duty,' but I should have kept my mouth tight.

'Anyway, earthquakes and floods,' I go on, 'let the rich guys build the houses for the rest, better, in a better place. Famines – more food. Wars – don't start them. You see, beneath it all, the love, religion, all that stuff, it's all quite easy. Fix it before it starts, you'll find the life-raft's stocked with goods, no meat, of course, or plants extinct – so on we float together, singing songs, until . . . It seems, they tell us – that the sea dries up. Or else it covers all. The struggle ends, we all go down, not accident, but suicide. Our fault, for sure – there's nothing to be done but wait the day. So – why bother, care – it all falls down, and there's an end.'

As I leave, my case half made, I hear them start – 'Arrogant and brash', 'obscurantist god-trampler', 'not at all our sort', 'crossed teeth are quite . . .' and I turn, make my mistake.

I give them all the finger.

Insults come fresh out the pot, they run with blood and gravy, parents and nation I have none, but if I had, their reputation's curried over, then, they bring on the gods with sticks and stones.

I stand at bay, but language fails, I dig my grave.

I'm not displeased to lose the job, and find I'm humming, 'Life is sacred – except in pursuit of justice,' It's quite catchy, though I feel it doesn't stop there. Pursuit when you're pursuing, or after too, when the quarry's down? Afterwards, is life sacred again, or when you do the justice? I feel it gives you credit for vendetta, – and is there something in there about honour? That's a sharper motivation than the search for justice.

I change my tack, and think, well, anyone can have tattoos, doesn't make them criminal, though it leaves you on the crest of something, wanting to improve what's been designed. Wanting to improve

– I've got this crazy animal, incised on my back, it's better than a monkey there, best I could do! I laugh. I'm still laughing when – here's Bella who denounced me.

'Good feisty response you made,' she says. 'To save my honour, I sought justice, but I should perhaps have punished you myself . . .'

'It's riskier, but more satisfying,' I say. 'They tell me "justice and mercy are one".'

'I wasn't thinking of mercy,' Bella says.

'The justice you do to yourself without mercy,' I say, 'that's the best kind,' but I'm puzzled, as the justice you do to yourself, it might suspend your sacredness, and the justice that the others do to you – well, that's their business, running away is yours. It's all quite complicated, but if it's about me feeling guilty as regards her teeth—

'No, not at all,' says Bella. 'Teeth don't come into it. It's changing the design, the aesthetics of what is, and so is meant to be.'

It's true, and as a painting or an installation, she's quite, well, '*bella*', but that's the word I

mustn't say, more indefensible thinking – and
justice here, it doesn't play a part.

Later, I hear her tell a friend, 'Glad I made that
head guy suffer. And the cash I get – maybe I won't
spend it on my teeth, it seems a waste.' The friend
agrees.

'Forget it, forget fucking teeth, and you and me!
It's not about that,' I shout.

I shouted . . .

Some echo! Where does the music go when you've
played it, heard it? That shout grinds me like a pestle.

'My tattoo,' I say, 'it's my shield, defence, a
creature, swirls part scorpion, and part cockerel.
Homage and protection, graven on the sacred body
– onlookers, turn to stone!'

Bella says, 'That tattoo quite puts me off.'

'No reason that you need to look. Forget
tattoos, just think how you betrayed me.'

We make a kind of peace.

We sit and puzzle over our difficult desires. The world, they say, gets smaller, everywhere the stuff's the same, parlours for straightening and for crinkling hair and ditto eye slits, hotels by the hour – if you can find the time. But if you have to go on foot, the world is goddam large, and keep away from where they grow the food, those fences sting like tasers, the guys with baseball bats will do you harm, so better find a job, walk on and find one, better than to be a stowaway. Besides, your life – it can't go on for ever, poorer you are the shorter it will be, though guys pretend it can be stretched. An infinite precariousness.

Those final days – the monkeys astride the burnished branch will throw you down a furry fruit that maybe tastes of lobster. Or else a Henry Clay. So, smoke till you puke, it makes no odds, and drink and ride in cars with fins like sharks', fenders of titanium keep you safe. And scream and laugh and screw, there's millions that are doing it, and millions looking on – in infinite compassion. It's your last day. So, leave your mark, your footprint, earth is striped with them, nameless it's true, but each a proof of some last fling, assertion, message. Finger in the face of something infinitely great, so huge it's just the backdrop, the radiation from a constant leak of energy.

'Don't worry, Bella. It will all end happily. Ever after too, I shouldn't wonder. I've all the feminine virtues, so I know.'

'I'm not worried. About anything. Besides, I'm not the one in danger, no cops are after me. I can go anywhere.'

Ah, travel! Now they're gone – those countries outlined with coloured pencils, armies in every shade of green-brown-grey, ladies with their ice-cream clothes beside rough beaches. All gone! Precarious, it used to be, like walking on glass roofs, but all too human. All different, and challenging, but now – a calm.

It's everywhere, one-coloured world, – the counting houses, temporary rooms where nothing passes over desks – pictures jiggling on the screens

– a hundred hundred lines to keep us in and punish.

'You're as good as a piece of toast,' says Bella.

Nothing to be said or added.

I say, 'Life passes one by. What luck!'

She peers at me, 'Maybe a little self-obsessed, even for a holy person.'

Fruit of someone's will – those women running from the fire, faces already running, skin stripped off, flesh all useless now. You have to give them peace, laugh at that will, to drive it out. Is it here, in wells, in caravans, the bowl of sky, in all their eyes? Or –

Is it all greed – and how banal!

Bella says, 'Moving around a lot, you don't feel like an alien. How'd you know anyway, how aliens feel? It's like they dropped you in an opera – there's no greeting there, just thirty warriors in cardboard, singing what is not a greeting, then other guys start popping at each other, some really die and others sing and sing, you need be twice as broad as life so you'll be seen. You're not part of the action, and it's all stereotypes, and down there, the pit, there's a clanging of pots and cymbals like hell's kitchen and beyond, a fringe of guys dressed up, an audience, a public – most just sleep on, but in the end they get their coats and clap long and some will even scream. You don't get paid. Why should you? You haven't sung, you've not been cued . . .'

She goes on, 'He took me to lunch, this big cheese – though I do know what real cheese tastes like, and it's not like he tastes – and we'd lots of stuff to drink, like mouth rinse, then I said, "Do we have to spend the afternoon with you poking about in my insides?" and so instead – we went to an art gallery. It was nice.'

'Good for you.'

'Those colours – magenta, umber, black silver, goose green – like walking through a city with your eyes closed.'

'Not all galleries are like that.'

'Well, it drew me in. I flourished.'

'So, you overcame that food and drink?'

'Yes, in a corner of the room. I'm sorry, but I'm not ashamed.'

'Somewhere there was a lack of tact,' I say.

'So right.'

'You may be a good girl, even daddy's girl, but fortunately there's only one of you. Generalised, life would be intolerable.'

'You can't live locked up in fables,' she says. 'I believe in living all day long – calls to prayer, if you like, devils, angels, everyone minding your business and you theirs, things all labelled in gold handwriting, not that squared-off print. Taking it all seriously.'

'Not for me, I'm afraid. I'm a citizen of everywhere.'

'Well, there we are.'

I wonder if she means 'we're the everywhere', or 'that's what divides us'.

Behind the display there's always something else, the something more I don't believe in.

'That "something more" – is emptiness,' I say. 'I want, I need, that emptiness. I am my empty shrine, my mystery, holy, all that stuff. No good watching me as I watch TV – you'll catch no subversive thoughts. My innocence is the black iron veil. Beneath the innocence, is emptiness, no tongue put out, no spit rolled round. My mystery is this – I love you all, brothers, sisters everywhere, I want you – not communion, but union. Yet – you bored guys, brothers, lookalikes, financiers before your screens – you think I'm plotting, know what evil is, or good. But – there I am: in contemplation. I love you all, all as you spy, distrust, and hate. I have no core, no hidden lymph. Love you, I hide nothing. Love you, my spare parts! But, in the end – we don't give trust.'

'But those guys are scum,' Bella says. 'You can't love them. The guys that sit and watch.'

'That's how it goes,' I say. 'What can we do? Those guys – they're so flawed,' and I whisper to her, 'They don't know what they're looking for. If they did, they'd do it. Transgress. But you see – this system – what makes it go and what will bring it down – is greed. Is wanting more than you deserve, than it can give. It's sucking till you're sick and what you suck is dead and dry.'

I feel the raft, raft of the *Medusa*, raft for we last two, is tilting towards landfall, some deserted place, some sand where we'll fight out our days – (Bella, you betrayer) – a scrapping and a tearing. Ritual duelling. Find a pole and push us off again, into the deep dark sea.

'Speak to me, Bella.'

'You smell of death.'

'Not mine. All those people round.'

'You take it all so personally.'

'And you betrayed me,' I say.

'I see that you deserved it. And maybe you wanted betrayal, like you hoped your friend did all those things – just by himself. Are you going to going to hold my treachery against me all your life?'

'We don't seem to have the choice.'

'How you preach,' she says, 'how you exaggerate. Let's go to a gallery, do something.'

'Bella, your rhetoric is your sweetest thing. But do I feel good, doing good to human kind? No – it's disgust, disgust they all lie down and die and suffer. They don't say nothing, coming from their scrabble in the fields and workshops, and over them is mister money . . .'

'Gallery,' Bella says. 'You don't need buy anything.'

I persist, 'Greed, Bella – just one sin of seven. You have pride, vendetta in your case. Lust is missing – but there are others. Idleness? Sophisticated accumulation? How does that sound?'

'Gallery,' hopping up and down. 'I need more rituals, more rituals – let's see some pics, a movie even,' and she pulls me.

'It's all a quest,' I say, being pulled.

'Lots of French names for what you feel, old slug. That's why they started guillotining. Off with his head, your head . . .!' and she capers.

'I always thought about the Revolution, that on balance . . .'

Maybe, again, in Africa, and Bella says, 'No,

China won't allow it.'

That day, balance was the last thing I should invoke. You don't have to buy anything. You lost me my job. No grudge. Is there?

'You must have wished for that,' she says.

At the gallery, she says, 'These are the tiniest things. Immaculate.'

'I can't see anything.'

'You must look real hard. That's the point, to see.'

'I know. But here there's nothing.'

'Some have gone for restoration,' she says.

I stare. Here in a corner is a bee, dead and natural.

She is chirping with delight, short cheeps of frolic and naughtiness.

The bottom of the display case – in the felt, there's a red blob. Manufacturing fault or just a sport. Nothing. Maybe a tiny silvered skull, or just a tear where something pinned was taken out. She's delighted, and I'm irritated. I say, 'There's less than nothing here.'

She laughs. 'You see, usually, when there's pictures, stuff, we just mooch round in silence, now we're talking. Talking aesthetics,' and she pauses like she's finding treasure at the bottom of a well.

'What's a dead bee cost?' I ask nastily, but she's pulling me on.

'Look, look, see!'

'There's nothing, and to imagine – why should I play that game?'

'There is, there is, there's so much – if you don't believe, ask him.'

She points to the guard in the corner, chauffeur's hat with that black cockade, mourning for someone in general. Fat-bacon face, pustules scattered delicately, a suit that smells of weekly cleaning, sweaty waiting-time.

'What do you know about something, fellow?' I ask him.

'Look deep,' he says, 'and when you find the smallest meaning, that will be yours, you fish it in, you capture it. Not the same catch as this young lady – look! she finds the little fishes everywhere! To each their meaning, and to each their penetrating gaze.'

I say, 'I just see the inside of my eyeballs,' and it's clear this guy's the artist, fabricator, and I see that on his coat it says he's 'Guide'.

Anger takes me at his arrogance, to take the credit for the guys who have to do the work, interpreting, fishing, falling in. I take him by his weak lapels, maybe it's a head-butt, not quite intended, rather, an aggressive slip.

His hat comes off, his bacon runs from fat to lean, and Bella says, 'Now there'll be trouble . . .'

'That doesn't cost me anything,' I say, but at once I know it will.

'Let's go to that' – a poster for a lecture, and she reads, 'Secret recipes: how Tibetan monks improved my baking.'

'It'll be a laugh,' she says.

'I don't laugh,' I say.

She's almost crying with irritation and frustration, pulling and pinching to liven me up, like a butcher primping a dodgy joint.

'Don't prod me!'

'You need it.'

'I've lived in hell and promised heaven, I've even built annexes to purgatory. Served up science, hired my spies, done crime and complicity, seen millions of naked apes in tents. Sex, love and death, it's all been jotted down, births too, though they're discouraged. Our primal customers have not made tools of stone because there were no stones. Nor bronze, because they mustn't excavate or start a fire.'

I mumble on, and suddenly, I shout, 'So don't push me under all this goddam traffic . . .' but she does.

There's my trouble – like I said.

I guess she's right, why should she waste an afternoon with someone who's just roadkill – and I'm hit, first in the shoulder, and I shrug that off, she does the penitent act – so, where's the fucking ambulance and all that stuff, and looking up at silly faces looking down, my legs are off on holiday, the arms are sullen, won't do what I pay them for, the head just comes and goes. It's just like switching channels and the same guys are all in different soaps, there's lots of snow, and someone says, 'He's dead.'

And someone else – 'no, he's just dying', and I think, oh fuck, those last words just escape me, but in fact I must have said them somewhere else, like 'naked apes in tents', that doesn't mean a lot, and I'm quite keen on meaning. Someone says, 'That's a good sign', though what they know about, or who they are, is far from me.

5 Dr Hani

I T'S LIKE I'm slowly turned to stone, and I think 'stone axes' – here comes the whole display of guys and gals, they need the territory, the tribes are rushing at each other, another accident, and club and smash – and where's the ambulance, as if that's got some cure. And now it hurts, but far away, pain leaves no memory, time no hurt, but history leaves its ache, you bet, and maybe that's my foot that's sliding into chronicles, or someone makes a sketch of me, using their fine opposing thumb – those little telephones can seize the moment, send it round the world.

I try to raise my hand, at least to give the finger, or just hide my face.

Now – here's a Dr Hani, filling up my skullpan with more cubic measures of imagination. I tell him, 'I've adjusted my past, my history, and come out altogether better – a real boost.'

'They'll think you're imagining it,' he says.

Good Dr Hani. Still believes that brain's the thing, improvement is the path. I say,

'Good Doctor, forget the brain, it's dictionary, not a story. I tried my best; perfection, self-satisfaction, were my goals, but now I'm moving on to evolution. I think art, religion, were spandrels, eyelids, as it were, for our third eye, wagging mechanisms for the tails that we don't have.'

'That could be fighting talk,' he says.

'Now, my brain size is right up. I think I've made the next step. I'm the first example of the higher kind of guy, leaving you neanderthals or sapiens, you wise and vertical ones, a space behind. So, you'll go on, you get to whittle stones, to kill some guys – better they're not in uniform – religious freaks will do, or anti-moderns, Afghans will do quite well for now, and then you'll find another bunch. But I'll have none of that. My path is higher.'

Dr Hani is intrigued, and shoots a syringeful of brain juice into his backside.

'I'll think of following you, my friend,' he says, 'I've got some terrible things I must adjust. Was some butchery, but not of people. When my past is clean I'll join you on the higher plane. But – I have one doubt.'

'Doubts are part of our humanity. So let's get rid of them.'

He says, 'They say we're at the Depthless Falls. Where the sick hippos stand, they feel their knees a-tremble, then let go and – WHOOOSH – over they sail, extreme sport ending in a cloud of spume. It's like you say: "We're on *Medusa*'s raft. Those less evolved, the clods, have just gummed up the sod we're circling on, with grease and soot and dust. We're done for, this restaurant ran out of food. We scoffed it up and now it's gone." So, there's the doubt – it seems it's all too late!'

I say, wisely, 'Medusa turned to stone – the message there is clear. Back to our stones, but then take another path, evolve. The only way to get a bigger, better brain, and . . .'

He's impatient. 'The raft is sinking too, my

wise old friend. The ship *Medusa,* like its patron, goddess, if it went to stone, it didn't have a chance. Stones often sink. And yet, the story's quite confused. Who magics who, or what? Maybe the ship sails on! Goddess and ship, it's all a mess, murder and suicide are one, you think, shipwreck, betrayal and enchanted shields, the Fall renewed and this time final – make up your mind, my dear old friend!'

He fixes me, he's confident, pretends he's puzzled, and goes on, 'But just believe me, if you can, the size of brain's irrelevant to this. The being all at sea! It's nature! Maybe we'll float on a bit, but in the end . . . The ship, like all those goddesses, just ended bad, now all ends bad for everyone. It always has.'

I must agree. 'In the end, dear Doctor, yes, the end's the end. But meanwhile, let's explore this other path that no one's ever taken, take samples – ah, the trees, the animals, flowers a-coloured like you've never seen . . .' and I go on and on, he says it's *fin de siècle,* that stuff, that what we need's some fart from sheep to power our cars, or weeds that burn for days. I tell him he should be mature, here is no wonderland, it's mud and fluff just like it's always been, but use our brains to find a way . . . Get off the raft, and not be turned to stone . . .

'Hmmm' says Hani, 'let's go back – art and religion. I commune daily with the "I" supreme – many times, some days. Some evenings, practise writing with a little bone and gold, the names of Same.'

'Then more fool you,' I say. 'That Being's just the higher stage, the one the current species, sunk in chimpland, has as its vague, its hopeless, aspiration. So too for art – it's pictures of a world that now your species conjures up – but you will never live in. It's harmonies one day will throng the inner ears of species new and better, books will have contents these men supreme will just intuit, no need to type them out and puzzle. The guys today – they're spandrels!'

Hani says, 'I'm proud you say I've glimpsed the future.'

'You ask what we shall do,' I add hurriedly, 'without that speculating, imagining, and all those fantasies of food and sex and sun and booze. Well, you for one can start to concentrate on making me feel better.'

He stares at me. I'm hoping for some sign. He says, 'Look out the window, you will see what they call a Facility. It's there the hackers do their alchemy. Yes, they read our thoughts and plan on who to kill or plot against,' and I correct him, though I haven't seen a thing,

'That would take a million years, and be so dull. There's heaps of stuff out there, you have to sift it all, it's like exhaust, they say there's bits of diamond in it, but they lie. For those who know, who really know – prime messages have a code, a T for truth. Real, true figures, messages or thoughts are coded thus – and all the rest is hokum, spit from agencies, spent shells that never held a charge. Find that T, you find the truth – each year, around the globe, there's maybe half a dozen T's: the lists, the ups and downs, who's pencilled in, who'll be rubbed out. The schema of the system, from its schemers.'

He's mightily impressed, but he says, 'You can't see in the windows, they're sealed shut and painted.'

Now, I stare at him. 'Just let me out this hospital. I feel like shit.'

'What makes you think you're in hospital?'

'The truck, that girl pushed me under.'

Hani beams, 'That's great, your paranoia's back. And as for getting better – well . . .' He stretches: 'The Cat,' he says. Gapes his mouth: 'The Tiger'. Already he's taller, fiercer. Elongates his neck and wiggles his nose. 'Giraffe and rabbit. You understand? You have to find your roots.'

'I like the rabbit bit.'

He points to a shiny cabinet marked 'Wonderland', and says, 'I use the pills they keep in there, when I feel down. A selection, wonderful things.' We take a few.

'I feel I've been done over by the cops,' I say, 'or maybe some Intelligence.'

'Those pills are costly,' he says, 'and you owe three fifty, cash and no hard luck.'

'The guys that picked me up took all my cash.'

'Well, that's not hard luck,' he considers. 'I guess, it's just routine.'

Another guy comes in, a miniature. Now Hani's stretched himself, we all seem puny.

'Here's Yusuf,' Hani says, 'he's my brother – blood's quite thick, you see, though not as much as you might like.' He pauses and continues, 'You see, I feel it very keenly – we from the East we're always being criticised or patronised – it seems that civilisation passed us by when you guys rampaged all over us, and so we didn't get the brains – inventing little telephones, speed dating, all those things. It seems we turned to stone. That's why it's so attractive – going back, to take another path, avoiding what you guys have managed . . .'

'That self-improvement spiel – it's had its day,' I say, without thinking too much.

'Self-improvement? It sounds like Bella – still calling her "that girl"? You idiot, just imagine –

we've tumbled out the womb in that dire camp you
say you built. Open our eyes, we think, "my God,
how wonderful, the tent, latrines and food in packs".

'For us inside, it's all fantastical, maybe a bird
flies over or a helicopter! Epiphany! For those
outside, like you – it's just the world turned upside
down. For us, inside, it's paradise. God put us in this
fantasy – at first it's rules and lots of blood and
punishments, then, the genre is fable, zombies,
missions. Well, that takes us . . .' he pauses, Yusuf
and I intent, though Yusuf's heard it all a hundred
times '. . . or it should, to where we use our brains,
our bigger ones, to start again, and end the madness,
discover "being in ourselves . . ."'

The chance, the hope, to start again, throw off
the bondage.

'Back' says he, and 'Forward' say I.

He's triumphant, and his plan is clear,
magnificent and visionary, though too late to save
us, anyone, I fear, and it's been tried a hundred
times. Just like the telling, all has failed, – it's just
another kind of pill for Wonderland.

Bella visits me, she bears no gifts. Since this is not a hospital, but just a place for feeling bad, or just inadequate, wrong kind of species – that is no surprise. What kind of gift might I expect from her? A box of tinies? Stuff found, unclassified? A flower found dead at dawn that maybe resurrects?

'You pushed me under a fucking truck,' I say.

She laughs, 'We were so excited, such a good time, and prancing down the street like we were king and queen, some midday with the people all around to cheer us on, the sun straight overhead, and you so keen on me!'

I don't reply, she's worked a tapestry too dense to catch another hook, my hook.

'Why?' I ask again.

'Just the way I am,' she says, she's proud of it.

If this is not a hospital, then I can leave, bearing a normal, incurable, but tolerable load of pain. I pass, but don't look at, the Facility.

Then, here's the club, here are the girls – the

ladies, women – in the cage as usual, they wear red skirts and whoop unevenly. They don't seem much like Bulgarians, though that's the theme. Then, they start taking off their clothes as usual.

I don't have a drink. The guys in the back room, watching through the door ajar, discussing taxes, kneecapping, no interest to me, I hear one, storytelling, 'Of course, he passed his lover's ruby on, his wife was mostly grateful, but at times I think she felt it was her price for his experience, so expert was he in smoothing things along, a dinner here, an introduction there – she must have felt cohabitation was all technique, a profession, the jewel a mortgage on his own performance, a payment that she held but not in trust, that could be passed along, a piece of banker's paper . . .' and on he goes, he opens up a world of springy prose, relationships that run and run, with second thoughts built in, and judgements made, remade, the values up and down as if they're auctioned through the years. Peace.

That is the trick.

I see Dr Hani from the street. He's sitting in a

white-lit basement. He holds a knife, on its point a large triangle of yellow cheese, he waves it emphatically as he preaches at Yusuf, who is silent. He's a triumphant hunting cat, with a hopeless mouse – who'll never get that cheese. Hani needs to make his argument over and over – but Yusuf too must eat, though it might be better to starve than have Hani always as his brother, his companion.

Hani's obsession takes me back – those Korean kids and I, running along the beach with arms outstretched like wings tilted for takeoff – wheeeee drawn from our mouths like ectoplasm. Thundering along the sand between the cliffs, the wrecking sea.

Bella cries, 'The opera, the opera! My sister Effie sings and dances too, maybe she's on – it's where they do all those old tales, courts and duels and armoured guards. It's our chance to run through those old emotions – honour, vendetta, transmogrification, all without us getting hurt.'

'Why not?' I say, 'I'd like to meet Effie.'

Bella goes on, 'It's right to take steps back. You know – like the Russians had to when they overspent, and now the Yanks have done the same, who knows where the steps retraced will lead – the robber barons and Wild West, they never buried those! Perhaps it'll be Indians and riding without stirrups? The Mexicans will make their move – d'you know how good their army is?'

On she capers, and I say, 'You're not as stupid as you sound, young Bella. Are you learning Mandarin or Hindi?' but she puts out her tongue and says 'old sourpuss', but I always knew our fear, trembling, sickness, call it how it feels, was part of waiting for another Genghiz, some new nursery punisher, doesn't give a damn for our fine feelings, doesn't even shunt us into camps before we're done for – on I muse, it's really not good dinner talk, it's really in bad taste, it sours the booze, and after all, my camps were there to ease the hurt, some reflection on the things to come, some partial burial of the pasts – it never works, the limbs stick out, you dig and dig, but they are deep within you, those cadavers never let you go.

'How about a movie?' I ask, hustling her along. 'There's warrior-action – *Warring States*; teenage love in *Troubled Times*; next week it's *Last Days*, three days only, and for kiddies *Chicken Licken'*.'

She's untroubled, says, 'I thought the last one was fast food.'

'Are you sure Effie's in the opera?' I say.

'Oh yes, she sings anywhere, she's a real nymph,' but I feel the sickness on me, and I say, 'I think I'm getting out of here, to somewhere. Quick. So if you want to come . . .' we talk around, Hani and I, he brings his atlas out, some pages blank, other scored through, and he says, 'I pray but don't have faith, so if you trust those little guys you voted for, then stay on here if not – I'll see you take your chance.'

'Some chance,' I say.

'That's the spirit,' he says and summons Yusuf, faithless hound, part wolf, part goat.

It's not my time, however, and I'll not stay with

them, nor yet with Bella.

I've business here.

I find a guy – I think he's drunk, and I am too. Let me be disaster made by God, since Man has made a lot. Almost all are manmade now, the water round your feet, the Lisbon earthquake too, no doubt. First time, the earthquake stopped us in midbreath, but we soldiered on. Now it's all been scheduled, there's no surprise, calamity's foretold and dated.

'Is this the best whisky you know?' I ask.

The label reads 'uisge-beatha-braiche: special bottle in Great Glens.'

The guy says 'yes', and I think but do not say 'Then more fool you.'

I drink the bottle, it is good, except they've mixed the booze with something else that's foul, and hard to separate. I take a careful aim and try to stand the bottle on a stump. Then, out my gun, the shooter. Try it.

Fuck, this doesn't work, I think. I've banged off all my shells, and nothing done. I throw the gun away and leave the empty bottle.

The cop can write a letter that's quite kind, bit legalese.

'You should have been a lawyer,' I say.

'Ah,' he says, 'So we have charged you?'

'I'm innocent,' I say, and so he says, 'We all are,' and off we go and chase this logic's tail a while. 'This shooter's yours,' he says.

'It was. It doesn't hit the target.'

'It's sure been fired a lot – it's nearly burned the hedge down.'

'You're supposed to find a cadaver for every shell that's empty,' I say.

'I know, I know,' but doesn't seem convinced. 'We'll look for them, don't fear.'

I tell him, 'I told you, this piece misses,' but he's set in track.

'If it's not you, the murderer,' he says, 'it could be some Gaelic wanderer by the look. We'll get you, and we'll find the bodies.'

'Maybe you won't find the one I hoped.'

'We count real good.'

He lets me go provisionally. The time has come to move along. Justice, mine, has not been done, and justice, his, will hound me. So, I take my leave.

Those scientists – they've given dates to all our futures. When we will burn, or drown, or suffocate. Why bother plodding on? The last days are upon us, we're the sheep, tilting our baas towards the thunder. Even the old sheep sniffs the wind, alert, and wants to join the lambs, trucked off to the butcher's.

I tell her, 'Bella, you're a sprite, a quite chaotic bunch of leaves and flowers,' and she laughs. Must keep her sweet, choosing this randoming person, hear her atonal chants to inconsequence . . . Maybe linking to uncertainty helps to shake off the cops. After all, your instinct tells you – stick to the raft: –

but this means you may be eaten by your shipmates, so the illogical course – that saves you – counsels sliding off. Just drop and float. The blue above, the blue beneath – do you hear the sirens? Are those mermaids rowing their golden barque towards you, deep bosoms leaning over, cradling you up?

'You catch my drift?' I ask.

'Honestly, I wasn't following.'

She's really honest.

'Hope?' she asks. 'No, I don't deal in that. It seems a rather nothing thing. As for the future, yes, that's a wonderful thing, you don't ask for it, or pay, but when you wake up – it's arrived!'

'Like a morning paper?'

'Only much better, and more interesting. Like pictures – they've no hope and they don't sell you future.'

Later, she says, 'That little map of yours, how we might be. It looks just like your camps, though it's a refuge – so you say. Where's all the masts, that stuff for wind, and spades for digging holes?'

'Those holes should save us from the bombs, if

we discount the pits for plague.'

'Latrines!'

'Of course! I hadn't really thought.'

'You should.'

'The only thing we can't foretell is – who'll survive these armageddons,' I say, and she says quite kindly, 'You needn't kill your friend – it'll all be done without your intervention.'

I say, 'These drastic times – quite take your mind off other things – now, they don't seem to matter snot,' and she runs on ahead.

'Let's make an excursion,' I say.

The water here is full of arks, some of tin and some of precious woods, some – brazen galleys, muzzleloaders poking out like heads. Some have pulpits at the prow, where guys with sacred books can bless or curse the waves, and some have nudes of gals or guys, some quite stylised, others chryselephantine, real or fake, so who's to tell. On each there is a film crew. Some sweeping nets aloft that scan for clouds.

On the plain there's villages, some like the one

I hoped to build, and guys are digging deep deep holes, as shelters or as plague pits, and those that haven't got their pass or permit just stand around, quite glum – the sea's down here, the sun's up there, both working as they're used to do, and Bella says, 'Those holes are far too deep.'

'Enlighten me,' I say.

'They need to dig latrines, or else they'll die,' and she's right, these people want to fool their destiny, and now they'll lose.

'Your village, is it a trip to future, or to past?' Bella asks.

The guys, busy as ants a-digging, or as coots a-sailing, – evolution working overtime, not to be laughed at. No animals in the arks, of course. I answer with a question.

'Well, Bella – are we diggers – or are we floaters?'

'If you had shot your friend, when you'd the chance, it wouldn't seem a justice. Annihilation . . . pouf!'

'He crossed a line.' Our friends cross lines – we

shouldn't shoot them all.

'I'm stardust,' Bella says. 'Read it in a book.'

'So, bits of you are millions of years old.'

She agrees, pleased. 'It'll help when I find my place, my own true place – maybe that's centuries old too.'

'I wouldn't look too hard – those old places are all over. The smell, the little rooms, the people, then water coming in, the mud . . .'

'You're so cynical for someone who's solved the problems,' she says and I think, I never solved a thing, just sometimes stopped the bleeding.

'As for real problems . . .' I tell her.

'You could send money like they ask.'

'Yes,' I say, 'I could.'

I tell my friend, 'I let you off, my pistol didn't work.' He laughs, then laughs again, derisively. He says, 'Lines are there, there to be crossed.'

'Justice is always there as well.'

'And now it's after you – you must hide well. Your cop is counting, every bullet means a corpse to him. You'll join the crowd, everyone is running round, fear for their lives, their future, most fear some judgment coming from the clouds, so you can hide among them as they scurry. And dig and sail. Salvation, but not rescue.'

He recommends me to a wise man.

The wise man says, 'I'm wise, it's true. But I'm not very wise. Earth, water, air, and fire – all a threat or a resource – they correspond to forest, island, city, desert. But I say to you', and he points, portentously, at me, 'Stick to the setting you know.'

'What, bars and such, and destitute people?'

'If it's that. There's areas of exclusion, chosen or not. You, for instance, are excluded from religion, wealth, and well-being. The lady here,' he points at Bella, 'is the lucky one – excluded from politics, and from dreams of liberation. Maybe just from dreams.'

'I have a lot of dreams,' Bella says.

'They don't count,' says the not-very-wise man.

I think – that wealth bit, that is Bella's fault. Then I recall my mission.

We come into this sort of bar, to rest our tired and indigested minds. On one wall we read, 'It's only outside because you see it inside your head,' and on the opposing wall, 'You only see it in your head because it is outside.'

'And here we are, in the middle,' says Bella. 'Some of both.'

This is a place where the dark angels come to smoke and sniff. Rest their tired wings and hide, tired of the questions, as they truck up and down the street. What a fucking job! Not for me.

'We're waiting for Effie,' Bella says.

Will she be in skins, or carried in, on a flatbed borne by goats and ocelots? Or good old dwarves, they know a thing or two from being on the downside, and at this instant I feel that we shall all be saved – Effie the singing ballerina, always on a stage, can't be for nothing, all that muscle tone and frocks she's been sewn into.

In she comes, alone, she's parked her court outside, the chariots with prows of ormolu, drawn by wild asses, and I hear the charioteers' tippytap outside, paid by the minute as they wait, every grain of life is counted as it spins away. It's right they tap their feet, their task to drive their queen from sister unto sister. Listen to those hymns, those curly trumpets blowing up a tempest!

Bella says, 'Hi, Effie. This is Effie.'

'I know.'

Seek out a Wonderland for the two black queens, Bella and Effie.

Well, it was all childish. The guns, especially the guns.

Effie says, 'That village – you planned it as all doghouses, but people like to live in towers. Look at the new cities, on the plain, all lookout spires and lighthouses.'

'Or else they burrow into kilns and furnaces,'
Bella adds, 'now making nothing, just fine thoughts
that wisp away – up the vents and chimneys, cooling
towers for thought, that spreads out . . .' and in the
plan we see the sheep, the foxes. In the distance –
camel trains.

'Don't take all these wise men too seriously,'
says Effie. 'You'll meet lots of them along the way.
The worst – the least wise – are those wearing tennis
shoes.'

'They aren't called tennis shoes any more,'
Bella says,

'The idea's the same,' I say. 'I'm glad that I've
renounced murder – not quite the thing.'

'You didn't renounce,' says Bella. 'You
screwed up.'

'Materially, it's the same.'

I'm pleased to say 'renounced', not pleased I
screwed up.

'What does Effie think?' I ask.

'Effie thinks of everything, like she's chewing

… She's a difficult case – our father sacrificed her, just to give himself a lift. Sent her on the stage to sing and dance. He was a sergeant, always off to wars, so needed space. And income. Precious things, those, for us, us blacks.'

'You never looked so black to me.'

'Your perception is your problem. Put what I say inside.'

So, we decide, we'll have adventures, seeking this or that, with no holds barred, nor declarations that we're interested in one another.

6   Travelling

WE TRAVEL everywhere, and –
'Not so fast!' says Bella.
We find no answers, find no movement
that isn't adding a storey here or there, a statue of
some guy now turned to stone or, rarely, bronze.
Roads for cars to trundle up and down. Lots of
camps. We speed up and down the red roads of
Africa, plunging down askew and sailing upward,
wings eager for takeoff. Roads of Russia too, still
the little huts called 'Restora . . .' something, 'closed
for lunch', that little chuckle makes your stomach
smile, and you're in peace a long stretch more.

Sometimes we see little bands, no longer
hauling barges, but waiting to be trafficked on, some
black girls waiting for their trucker who'll explain
the mystery. Lots of places turned to stone and
staring out, and we forget we're fleeing, as we seem
the one thing that's in motion not in chains – must

hurry on, some collapse might be about to happen, but you wouldn't notice. Some places there are animals, kindly pottering along the streets, and others – there is nothing. Weeds or bushes, someone gathers seeds, you never know, and 'Why don't they bury dogs that's smashed?', and on and on, what little sensibility you have is spent in changing tires, turning the wheel – that old Camaro's like a souvenir from home.

'Think of it so,' Bella says, 'the great leap was to come together, live in camps, like that is all there is. Some camps is tents that blow away, and some of breezeblocks that gets shelled, and some has neon in and out, some sound trumpets from the battlements, some has a muezzin that says how it can all be right. A bit of discipline, of squaring off. The new world – would be the end of huts and cardboard slums – just come together into camps! To pass the night. Our best heavens – try to avoid the ones that kill you quick, and try to build the camp that keeps us really safe . . .' and she looks at me, as if I have the plans.

The guy in the white dustsheet says, 'We had here,' and he waves towards the thorn fence, 'a centre of fine learning, people came from all over, not just the Arabs who went away and left their God – it wasn't desert here, but University.'

He pulls us through some tiny rooms, where paper plugs the roof against no rain – paper from a universe, paper from plants, from animals, people even, illuminated and primped out, first letters like a guardhouse – 'are you fit to read the text?', pass first the scrutiny of God, whichever one, and 'who the fuck are you, anyway,' but, 'Knowledge,' says the guy, 'What'll we do with it?'

We shuffle through our stereotypes, and he goes on, 'Some conquerors – they didn't even have a decent map. That Genghis Khan – he just went on and on, just territory full of folks with skulls to bleach. Take India, those Hindus had it right, they didn't put the dynasties and viziers and queens in synchrony, in diachrony – just the stories were the thing: weak king on quest, kills some monsters who're unarmed, maybe eats his children who he's never seen, boiled up in some stew – must have been pissed to have done that – conquers some princess who he's never seen before. You catch my drift?' and now there's crowds of us, and we say 'yea', and then he says those tall poppies were really repressed gays, instead of rampaging and killing folks, should have sorted out desire for bedroom games.

'I love gays,' Bella says, 'they make the world go round. If gays are gay, that is – the solemn ones are just a drag.'

The lecturer, the guy, goes on, 'It's not all sex, of course, although to pump up your own land by adding bits and people who don't want – it's all to do with bedroom. You guys out there,' he waves a hand, 'elect those twisted people who can't just say their piece quite straight, unaided – no, they put on those old tall actor's boots, the better to be seen, and spark the crowds, and round will throng the snappers and the slappers,' and he's steaming on, and we are running on ahead, the words are wonders, and we see a mist is lifting, rocks turn into sheep, the heather smells of lilies, and in the grass you spot cornelians and a solidus or two. He stops.

'What's to be done? Nothing, I fear. You clods.'

Bella says, 'Wow, I really enjoyed that – vision and insult all in one. It makes you glad and sorry that you are what you are.'

She confides, 'You should walk before you run away, and sure, she's got a shattered life, our Effie, that is what they say,' – but being tied to me is no salvation, maybe I'm sorrier for her than me.

We pull a scam to get some cash, we need it, so tough luck on who's the poorer, and I say, 'Money is made to circulate, that's why it's round, the world's made in its image – took a while for guys to see that everything is circling round and rushing outwards, into nothing in particular or who knows what – the infinite inventiveness of stardust till it hits the back wall.'

Bella does a little dance and says, 'I know, I know, I'm stardust,' and we're on our track again.

We should have seen strange things. A whole continent run past. Tigers, I suppose. Instead, this storehouse of unused talents, unusable and into frustration – avoid your suffering, dump it on the rest.

'What does it all mean?' asks Bella.

'You drive now, but go fast.' Then, I add, 'We've never been here before.'

Bella says, 'And yet – that job, you were responsible here, and here's where I was born, perhaps.'

This jagged relationship changes all we see, and I forget that somewhere there's a search for five or six cadavers – not my responsibility . . . on we skim, it's dust and thorns. 'Run, rabbits.'

Now, in the dusk, a clearing – down there a stink of kerosene, a dump of shacks, a city, and up here there's music and some dancing. Guys have gathered, no beads and feathers here, though the white shirts is most of what you see of them, they've thrown their tools – some staves and binbags, briefcases – in a heap.

'I want to join them,' I say, and the dance is hotting up, but Bella stays.

'I don't do other people's ecstasy,' she says.

Soon I'm dancing in the dark. A slack huge drum goes wump wump wump, and we go stamp stamp stamp, just letting it all off, although I see I'm in a little space all by myself. And then I see a line of shirts, a-going up to heaven, slow – and then I see it's up a ladder – now, I pick it out and hear another music. Not heaven, but a dark fuselage on stilts, a keel – it's a vast shebeen in the sky! And now I see the stars, not in the sky but on the promenade, they're sequined backsides changing shapes, the silver and the gold flash out. It's women, dancing, entertaining. But I don't go up, and on we drive.

'Faster!' I cry, and Bella plunges down a slope and in the curve we roll, frisky old car, rolls like a mare on grass. It doesn't lose its pieces, and our heads go round and round, and ah! the energy, and as rotation slows I feel electric juice has spread all through me. I'm done with running, done with tippytoes and saving souls (or shooting them), and then we stop, quite upside down.

I say, 'Hey! That was some ride!'

She laughs, and says, 'I'll show you! This is running!'

And I think, Thank you Bella.

I'm innocent again.

MEDUSA II

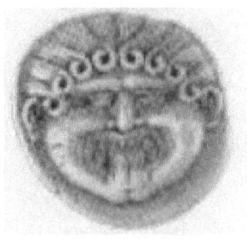

7   Home

WE ARE home – not mine. There is Dr Hani, whirling a spoon round a cauldron that goes wump wump wump. 'Peace!' Friend!' he says.

On the wall I see a parchment – he has a doctorate, University of the Sahara, in cooking mushrooms.

'I love culture,' he says, and his tall white hat, like a dervish's, spins round and round, 'And I love mushrooms.'

The little heads are yellow, gold, red and brass just sliding into green – they leap in a froth so white, it could be some horn, some metal. 'Mmmm,' he says, the handle of his ladle still has leaves – or maybe they are growing fresh?

'So many cooks,' he says. 'Don't really like the cooking, it's a kind of rendition of the cultures, of things found, kidnapped, and then mashed. But – I

do love the cultures, make them seethe together –
here, gathered, treasured, from caves and grottoes.
You have to read to them, if you're a master. Light a
single candle, and they'll lean towards you, on their
leg. They have to make the sacrifice, but do so
gladly, no regrets. No illusions, mind – you don't
make art, you make a stew. And eat it – mmmm.'

It's Bella's home. It's a house of the Sixties.
Each dweller has a room – the music falls around
like snow, some celestas, stride piano, anxious
youths in love, choirs of horns – it's all there, like
Vienna before it soured. Then, at midnight, all the
doors are locked, whoever is inside. At seven all
awake to birdsong, some of it mechanical.

It's quite like Hani's stew.

He goes on, 'Some of these—' and he points to
the coloured knobs bobbing in the froth (so white,
Saharan bones or Chinese white) '—are blood-fed,
undersides of altars from old Mexico, some from the
caves of Malabar,' and he winks at an Indian lad,
who yawns and wrinkles up his nose.

'Old whitey Forster,' says the lad and would

proceed, but Hani flourishes with, 'Some from the steppes – how they cluster round the graves! – and some quite innocent, where the poplars grow and wave – so tall, like masts, green sails a-furled.'

'He's a great kidder,' says Bella, showing me more people, 'My family. We're not related, quite by chance, just like real generations,' and there is Effie, unattended, in fluffy slippers.

Blowing up the embers, there's Yusuf, and I think, Here's a bunch of guys I've seen before, but really, they're as random as you'd wish, or as you'd have to meet. You find your raft, you hope they're vegetarians, your castaways – with some we'll drift, and others have those little glasses, to spy with – we'll make landfall on some goddam patch of sand, all pearl and abalone, some poisonous pigs there on the beach – and even found a cult and dance around, and the mushroom broth is going wump wump wump, – and anger's there, but there's no tree where you can cut a spear, and on I muse, the guys are hungry.

'Not yet, not yet! Not ready yet!' Hani says,

'Some fine talk, hurry it along.'

'It's not people that I mind,' I say, 'it's language. Language gives justifications, lays emotion on the things, and differentiates them – it's a great invention, but it binds us into bands and people we don't like, and into rituals we'd better not perform.'

'Sure!' Effie says. 'One day we'll all be tall and lithe, and dance, maybe we'll sing songs without words – and celebrate our seven types of silence,' and inside we cheer, we don't communicate too well not having common tongues, and ourselves not common types, we circle round, try to explain, but who knows what and – 'Isn't it ready?' asks Bella.

'Absolutely not yet,' says Dr Hani, and I think, the white – could be abalone shell, mother of pearl, a mixing of the elements, or mist on rice fields, the little enamelled frogs, they sing a six part song, according to their size. It's all so wonderful, the mushrooms take their time, the beauty of it all, ourselves, it brings a tear, but we are goddam hungry. Yusuf has given up, and goes to bed, there on the hearth. He smiles and sleeps, he's maybe in the caves, gathering this magic stuff, humming quietly, not a word.

Up and up, 'Don't count the floors!' says Effie. The mist is seeping in like ivy, silver and white, we open a door, and there's a bush – it might be khat, maybe it's Christmas somewhere, behind the bush a guy with scissors. Then we see it, not a moving wall, and not a frieze, it's a town, he's made with paper, pastels, then photoed it, yellow and river-mud, some grass in ruts. A garage, though there's two guys here on bicycles, the sign says, 'Am a Trans – am man/wom-an', and there's a row of them, the cars, red, gold and black. Some palms, some have their arms quite withered, house with black window holes.

'It's beautiful,' I say.

And Effie says, 'He's making pictures of a town, he wants some guys to rocket it – you know, you put these pics on line, and some big cheese is told, they think those things in there,' and she points to some brown tubes, they could be trunks of trees or sewer pipes, 'Are rockets too. And so, with luck, they'll send an army in. They try it all the time, it's called intelligence.'

I say, 'It's awful,' and she looks at me and does not speak. 'It's out of the character of the house,' I say, and we hear a chant. 'Baby, burn me to the bone, I won't pass this night alone!' and she taps her foot, tries a shuffle, says, 'They're not really part of us. It's so high up, you see.'

Effie squints at me. 'You don't really mean "awful"?'

'Routine, then. Professional. I'd even buy one, quite innocently. Beautiful.'

'The photos are massive, but the miniatures are, well, quite tiny.'

'Are there really new Transams in a line somewhere?'

'It's to make the Americans feel at home. Chinese feel envious. Besides, you've no cash since

Bella got you fired.'

'That's a part of Bella, she's like that. There's nothing between us – on the contrary. We thrusted through Africa.'

Effie says, 'I respect you for that. Bella was scared.'

'Nice people, dangerous place.'

'Almost a new life for Bella.'

'I don't believe in new lives, do you?' I ask, wanting to find out about Effie. 'You're such modern people for this Sixties house – I'm not used to you close up.'

She laughs. 'Who are you used to, then?'

'Disasters, mostly. People going back to basics, probably not far away from that already.'

When do we eat, I think.

Effie says, 'That Dr Hani is a tease – if it doesn't turn out right, he feeds it all to Yusuf, and we're off to bed without,' and she laughs again – 'He's a professional too!'

Yusuf had all our dinners.

The wind wheeled round our tower all night, snow came and thawed, it was gothic, and the sisters, Bella and Effie, slept, and Robert Mitchum didn't come, and though the house is Sixties, no one here, now, would recognise him. Locked in, we are, and safe, safe though it's all a little improvised. Our cosy camp, warm in a continent, a century, of camps, wavered a little, as though it couldn't hold its edge, its matter, and, when we couldn't sleep, we thought of moving on; our complicities, murders committed or proposed, weighed lightly, if at all, and we arose like new men and women of a wiser age.

Oh no, I thought, as Dr Hani stood at the ready there, a kind of pitchfork in his hands, tormenting mushrooms.

He says, 'I don't do leftovers,' and I say, 'That's good, I'm off,' – the musics start, the floor above creaks to *pliés*, somewhere a concertina band is splitting into sixteen parts, someone has erred and hired a double section of trombones, and in the anger rising there's that goddam drum, it starts its wumping, and I grab the sisters.

Dr Hani follows when he's kicked at Yusuf curled in the ashes, blissful.

'Work on your memories, you guys,' he says. 'No good just remembering, you must make them over, exchange.'

'And a bigger brain to you!' I say.

He doffs his white hat in mockery, and I see inside it there's a kind of steel bowler, the newspaper says 'millions of refugees, government denies responsibility', and a little of this, it really does you good, at least they're too many of them for a camp, and maybe they can found another state and borrow food and water from a neighbour.

'Come on,' Bella says, 'you're good as toast. I'm hungry, let's forget that stuff and ask our friends for work.'

'Good luck with evolution,' I say to Hani as we leave.

He says, 'Those brain boosts were just cosmetic – it's occurred to me, that bigger brains need bigger heads, that's harder to procure. I'm changing tracks.'

To console him, I say, 'There's lots of universities that need a guy to teach them mushrooms.'

'Universities,' he says, 'nah! Those tiny offices, all that begging for cash – I'd sooner work the street. And by the way,' he sees Bella and Effie leaving with me, 'don't ever marry one of those nymphs – be like the gods, at least, the successful ones. Just visit once and then move on – a thundercloud, and turn them into something if you must. But not a quest! It isn't worth it,' and he gives me benediction with his fork.

'I wouldn't dream of it,' I shout back, 'besides, under that truck . . .!'

'A passing incident,' he shouts back and then the guy who does the photos for intelligence – he hustles past, and says, 'We need an emirate – those Northern guys are proud to have a continent with all their stuff to sell – so proud with just their stall, a souk! Well, we can set up our own, we've more ideas than them,' and when he's gone, the Doctor says, 'There's mostly guys here unemployed, that's working for intelligence,' and when I ask, 'Is this house yours?' Effie is close and hushes me. I think she whispers, 'Finders keepers,' but I can't be sure.

'If it's money you want,' Effie says, 'I know where there's lots.'

'The kind in little bags, a-jingle for the stage?'

She doesn't smile.

'The police are watching me,' I say.

'It's their profession.'

'They interpret things – things you may not have done,' I say and hope.

'Well, you can go and hunt for Hani's mushrooms,' she says. 'Or you can be with me, follow my plans.'

'What do we tell Bella?'

'She wants to know what's useful, not what you might want, or plot. I can assure you, that mystery stuff's not worth a spit with her. If she wants to dance, she will.'

'That's your profession too.'

She's irritated. 'I do it in time, in tune, with other people, and the others pay to watch.'

'Will you be watching when I get the money?'

'Forget your friends, politicos,' she says, 'forget the millions that they set in motion – those people dead, armed, or fleeing. Forget the books they write when they are lurching to their deathbeds and may say – "mistake", or "looking back". They don't look back – they're dealers. Make a deal, a trade, and call it a decision. Spoon in a little this, a little that, and stir, and bubble. Don't expect regret or justice – it's not that game.'

'I'm not the person to do justice,' I say. 'I just try to punish – and if it's money that we're after, even that's irrelevant.'

She's impatient. 'Bubble, bubble – forget your Dr Hani, mushrooms, brains and all, you're in my crew, set to, and hoist my sails!'

'Are we reduced to this, the quest for money?' I

say, and I think, my raft is thin on talent, we're too specialised – there's Hani, and the sisters, Yusuf who eats and sleeps, the guy with miniatures – spy or terrorist – some cops, no doubt, assassins various. Too many for the nothing that we'll have, no one to find a star and steer.

It's clear to me, 'We need a politician to talk us through.'

'Don't even think!' Effie says. 'We'll need to cut in everyone!'

'I know a politician who's no good at anything,' I say, 'we'll pick him up from exile.'

'A woman would do just as well,' Effie grumbles, but I have my way.

Paco the politician says, 'I'm not much good at anything. But I need to rest my feet. Your raft will do.'

'The raft for now is just a metaphor. We have to wait until the stone ship sinks.'

'A metaphor will do me just as well,' he says, 'I've experience of ships of stone, or craft that do not move. They all do sink, if you can't push them along.'

'First, we must find some treasure,' I say. 'Not on an island, there aren't that many left,' and he says, 'That's fine, the water swirls the cash around, to each what he or she deserves.'

I slide the poor disastered people, almost safely, onto my metaphor, where –

Hani guards his worn tureen, inside must be – since he's said he doesn't truck with leftovers – fricassée of brain, to help us out this alleyway of fright and fraught. I see him writing in his notebook, 'First reaction, panic', and I think, it'll not be long before he slices layers off our revolution, our salvation plan, and calls what's left, altruism.

I hadn't thought – in metaphor, the sea is purple, froth from the waves is luminescent, clings to our hair as we hold on, the waves are metres high, and each a few centimetres apart, it seems to me they groan, the water's thick with everything it broke, with limbs and fur and horn, whole roofs, divans, – those birds are black like vultures and they swoop, and Bella scrutinises this promiscuous broth, it's full of ground-up things like beaks, and humps much bigger than our platform is – machines of plastic, canvases of naked flesh for sponsors with a million bucks.

'All inhuman life is heaving up beneath us!' she shouts, and there's Effie! – is that a sail she's raised, to take us to no place, or is it just the muscle of her voice, bellowed above the storm, red folds of guts and throat, a Flying Sister, banned from every port and reaching none?

Then I remember – Hector, the Boss, Franco the dealer – I didn't let them on – but there they are, a-struggling in the soup, both cursing me and praising, with vows of hatred and of loyalty – reluctantly we pull them on – it's really very small, the bottom of a plywood shack, of course there is no useful detail here, of how to steer, or where? or what?

We just cling on, try to postpone the cannibal time, and Yusuf sees he'll be the first, an inconsidered morsel to be eaten raw, maybe a little salt! The spy photographer has gathered in some tiny heads, not needed on this voyage, so he says, and makes a miniature for us – no, wait, the miniature is us, he slips it in a bottle, maybe the one I practised on to help my shooting dead my colleague, friend – who's now beside me, and he has a list of things he says he fears I did, the thugs paid off, or put on payroll, things that we humanitarians do, and screw the humanists, it's all in context – if there isn't any, then do the first thing that you can that no one will find out.

Here is Paco, politician, and he wants a list of who shall have their rations first, and I must tell him – here, we're on a metaphor, we didn't pack on board some food or water, though the water's here all right, it makes a roar so's we can't hear delicate thought and fine distinction, and there's no mast nor anything to tie us onto, and I think we'll first start letting go, not even think of eating Yusuf, nearer my god, and ancient mariners are not the things that come to mind, and Effie shakes me, and she snarls – 'beneath your fooling fantasy there's too much goddam realism' – and Hani's looking sick, he's dropped his notes, the brains have slopped away. There's shouts and shooting, Franco's cutting deals, the Boss would have us walk the plank and Bella's in an ecstasy at all the froth and little bits of lighted nothing on her face.

I have to bring some order here. 'You guys,' I shout, 'we're really shipwrecked now,' and Hani mumbles that he's called his notes *The Extinction of the Species*, and it's true, if evolution won't go back and start again, there's nothing says it must go on and on – and one day reach a landfall.

The setup is collapsing. We risk all being swept – off the raft for sure, into that lumpy vertical sea – off the map, where no one's looking for us, where we don't quite exist, but yes we do, already we are fighting, saying goodbye to little lives we're quite attached to. Though of course, the lives – they could be better, more consistent if they're going well, less so if not. Effie and Hector in cahoots, and my own hand on the inexistent rudder, what a bustup, what a conflict, our values like real swords in Chinese opera, the personalities, Effie's voice that rears up and out, huge tarpaulin smothering us. At the last, I end the metaphor. I save us all, to sail another day.

Long ago, a year or two, when we didn't know we'd turned our world to clinker, there I am, sitting beside my friend. Botching up a new disaster area, disposing of the stranded souls.

'They don't want us here,' he says. These people could have passed so easily, from a tradition, mild, declining, to some cooperation. Instead, in came the wolves, the greedy, brutal ones. And we – we loved them, then we hated them, but armed them too, the

wolves.'

'Whoever wins, they'll throw us out.' I say. 'We're in the wrong, it's all illusion. We didn't offer something we called modern life – we just brought them emergency, brutality old style, and greedy guys here, everywhere. And we're corrupted too. Some just stay stupid, but most must cut a deal.'

We're not quite volunteers. We're paid, quite well, to patch them up, or make some stuff to sell. And then we hand them back. We come to fix, and screw it up...

We scrutinise each other, I and my friend, to see who oversteps the line invisible – irrevocably.

We sat there, two imperial colonels, melancholy, wise, we'd subdued a native people, humankind, and now a bit regretted it. What idiots.

The husbands smiled at us, said, 'hi!' when we're in earshot, who knows what brutes they were at home. Humans for ever perking up or sobbing, this river dries, that desert blooms, here they take slaves, there, there's a trade in salt and guns. Vanity's a dark inviting cave, it runs and runs deep in the mountain till you can't get back, and settle down to cut some

animal in the rock or draw a devil that some others
take to be your last, your hopeful, message.

'We've screwed up each others' lives,' I say to
Bella, 'and now should look for some more
permanent place. That house that Hani's squatted in
– it seems a shade precarious . . . but our choices are
quite small – there's trade that we could try, and
offices that do a business that you'll never fathom.
There's sweeping and there's digging, maybe some
hammering too, or pouring, walking up and down,
and being butlers. We could try elections, or a
brothel, planting stuff or pulling weeds, or milking
this or that, or sticking needles in and burying if you
can't.'

And in the end we both decide – we're looking
for security, so we'll be guards, be mercenaries.

We recruit ourselves.

It's like a tent, but made of marble, with canvas on the floor. Screens with globes that twirl and spurtle, puffs of gold and purple, the business, – wars, incursions – doing well.

'It's wonderful – a soldier's life for me!' Bella says – she takes a wheel, it spins, and suddenly we're in a screen, we're on a mountain path, a tree, a snake – no, it's a tail, maybe a puma's tail, and there we are, Bella and I, loping along, unarmed it seems – like the mock king and queen at midday under the lime trees, seventeen, with every care upon us, borne lightly, and with all the rest to come – and far below, a clearing, the red-brown-ochre bodies, Catherine wheel of flowers, and pumas lying in the shade . . .

'That's us!' says Bella, 'Like we're having a good time, a pity that's it's you with me, but still...'

'Bella,' I shout, 'they're recruiting us, the movie isn't real . . .' but off she runs and sings a song, 'A Soldier's Life for Me', and guys in violet

uniforms with silver plumes are watching us, at her
they smile, at me they scowl, they think we're
intimate or at least in confidence. We're young and
light, that sun is overhead, I think I see some dams,
that river's dying and I see the last fish flapping out,
yes, there's a sign, 'Respect your nature' and below,
smaller, 'life is short'.

It's all banal, but here we're safe, the other
guys, real warriors, get massacred, but we are
counted if we fall. They'll give us bits of uniform, I
know that at the start it never fits, there's stuff from
someone else, maybe the pants aren't there, or belt
and boots, 'just put the bullets in your pocket, we'll
sort you out tomorrow', and here's a gun, you try it
out, and now you've got the most secure assurance
that exists – and even safety if you miss or hit the
wrong guy, or lose your balance, kill someone or
maybe even worse – but we are safe. Safe as you
can get.

'When you've shot off all your shells,' I
whisper triumphant to Bella, 'just take the cash,
you'll find it lying round, or coming in, in

planeloads or on camels . . . This is eternity, the
eternal craft of save yourself, – until some accident
or officer vainglorious or paid off, some incident,
will maybe put an end . . .'

'There is no end,' the Major says. 'So serve and
serve until you drop, and when you drop we'll pick
you up, into the vertical once more and never feel a
thing,' and Bella asks about the rooms – 'Don't
want a bunkie, never him,' and she points at me, and
I think that's out of order, but this young hen, the
Major, says quite prim, 'We're not savages. Sleep
with whomever you wish,' and Bella's pleased.

We've got ourselves recruited. The guy – who is a
gal – has no cigar, but calls to mind the Boss. She
says, 'Hah! Looking for the safest option,' and she
doesn't laugh, and there's equality, so I and Bella
can enrol in the same unit, same privileges, all of
that.

'We're very normal people,' I say, and our

officer looks pleased.

'That's the best sort,' she says, though I admit I have a plan to see if we are normal, or just extreme, and as if she sees right into me, she says, 'The concepts shade, they make a fine shade of ordinary,' and Bella says, 'I like a sharper colour,' but the Major doesn't pause, and says, 'You may have heard, they say, "we give protection, but at times we may exact Protection!" Quite untrue! Our main aim's this: to keep the world a-turning round, with no apocalypse, no slithering out of orbit, implosions, stuff like that. We act according to the rules of common sense – survival.'

When she hears, 'You found it!' Effie says, 'I told you there's a lot of cash just waiting for you, shares for all, and all in line with common sense,' and Bella makes a face, 'I want the choice of who I share my room with,' and it's true, hers is the hope we have that stands above the truth, or justice, religion that's revealed or may be, wait and see, all that.

Effie goes on, 'The perfect thing for people

without qualities. Hired guns, they call you – and at least you're armed. It's a fine tradition – gather up the slaves and make them into bodyguards – a classic shift. I'm so happy for you both.'

I tell Bella, 'Effie must love you, to send you under arms.'

Bella says, 'These pants go round twice.'

'They must be mine – this tunic's surely yours. Give me your boots.'

'You can't order me.'

'Sure I can,' I say, 'I'm your boss, I've got more plumes.'

'An accident.'

'Which of you drives trucks?' the Major asks.

'I do,' I say, and Bella pouts and shakes her head.

When we're alone, I tell her, 'You say you do, then you find a mate who tells you how. Besides, this army, militia, gunmen – they're all alike, they bust up stuff, their own is first to go. You do it so's to get something better. Or if you're carrying stuff – a lighter deal.'

'Well, you know everything – tell Dr Hani, he's our cook,' she says.

'I doubt it!' I say, and indeed he says, 'No cooking! I'm your psychiatrist, so when you kill, I make you feel real bad. Cut out the funny mushrooms stuff – these are my people that you're hustling into,' and of course, he knows where we are going – now, he admires how Bella wears her plumes.

'You're in this for your safety?' I ask. 'The safest place there is?'

'The opposite,' he says. 'My project's still the observation of us all, as if we were evolving on a raft. This is a smaller scale, more concentrated. More extreme.' He adds, 'I love extremes. You guys will think you're safe, surviving as you will: but I see something else. Your evolution – that will suffer,' and I think that maybe his whole houseful – the bandsmen, the guy that's into Terrorart, Yusuf the innocent – our comrades all! – will join the company. A little band of musketeers, of horsemen too, we're marching, riding, wherever we're protected;

terrorise the terrorists, honour the strong, escort the powerful, rob with discretion, and avoid the poor.

'My uniform's all scratchy,' says Bella. The colour doesn't suit. The cloth is used to cover pool tables – we could have been in peach or apple green, blood red or black, but violet seemed appropriate, and Bella fusses, criticises. We have lectures – though no one, ever, tells me how to drive my truck, my Mack.

We're told the ways to blow up houses – the artist's useful here – to drive off livestock, how to tell what's sheep and other, how to pick up suspects, how to torture, and the Major says, 'You'll find the population's hostile,' and I say, 'That's a surprise,' and Hani says to me, 'You'd better just take notes – your way, you'll lose your plumes.'

Sometimes we march up and down, the bandsmen play *marches militaires* that come from hell, they've had to change their instruments, and raucous lads, paid soldiers, come to stare and sneer – the 'desert violets', or 'the Shrinkers' we are called.

'Can we shoot them?' Bella asks in fun, but they're an enemy we don't shake off, although we try to shoot to kill, there's always more and more of them.

The lecture that we all admire is Dr Hani's on cosmology. He scoots around the legends, the stone ship, *Medusa*, then the stout elephants who we hoped would bear the globe's weight, and the questing and the quarrelling, when families were large and guys were weak, adventurers, and monsters all identified in caves with labels and their vulnerable spot marked out.

'Remember,' said the Major. 'The bad guys here will try to harm you, but next door we've done a deal, and other bad guys there are "kind of" friends. It's rather complex – best advice is "shoot

first", and don't be fooled. Even a guy in violet –
may not be one of us but just some dude gone
clubbing, same goes for the soldiers – remember,
"shoot first" and say you challenged.

'Worst of all, the people here tell lies. They try
to do you down, to hide the truth, no matter what
you do. It pains me, guys, but you might say, we're
not so popular here, although we try to save them
from themselves, send them to school . . .' and Bella
whispers that she hated school, 'real dullsville',
says, 'All this religious stuff, it's just like school –
I'm looking for a fresh direction, something to hold
to – hate the sea, the tilting up and down . . .'

The Major doesn't understand, she says, 'One
last thing – this religious stuff – you'd better just
keep quiet, and if you've faith, then sit on it, just
keep it shut.'

Hani objects, 'Then what . . .?' and lessons are
all over, Bella wants conversion if it's better than
the thing she's got, the Major quietly seems to say,
'They're worse than us, and serious about it,' and it
seems I'm back again to tents and camps and people

hoping that they'll resurrect, go on to build some huts, and quarrel, maybe have a singsong in the sun . . . but here – it's all security, especially our own, they pay us and we count the notes, the ink's still wet and Hani says, 'I'd sooner have it all in coin, in gold, if that is possible . . .'

The Major says, 'The motto's "finders keepers", and besides, there's entertainment coming' – and of course, it's Effie, sings some arias by Egk that leave us cold, and does a little dance of death that cheers us up because it's done so delicately – Salome to trombone accompaniment, and even Yusuf says for him this is eternal art, and we're all proud to think our culture wafts us here, saving these guys just swarming round, their dirty looks, their lies, prevarications, some cant they've learned from Calvin, we've no doubt, and Effie says, 'You people make me proud, and Bella's plumes look lovely in her hair,' and then she's off, she has a little case for cash, but does a deal with Hani – and it seems that gold is still the best, if you've got lots.

8   Escorting

THEY ALL come, in every size and every tongue – they're our escorted ones – discuss the sheep and goats, the treasure that there is or had been here. Every person has a plan, and every person has an escort. It's not quite paradise, but every Violet does what he or she prefers. A woman, local as we call them so, she asks me, 'Why you here and when you leave?'

'We're here for our security,' I ask. 'We do just what we want. And when we go – you'll do exactly what you want.'

'Some doubt would do you good,' she says. 'We had another guy who did exactly what he wanted, he and his. When you've gone, another bunch of guys will do – unless you kill them all – the same. It will be good, we'll prosper, gold coin will circulate. Our children will be doctors, maybe lawyers, some will be shot on rockets, discover new worlds up there,' and to cut her short, I say, 'Don't overdo it, here there's only goats and sheep, weddings and burials – you should get tourists, otherwise, my good woman, here nothing's worth a spit.' I hurry on.

'Rigour!' says the Major.

Outside there is a calm sea of people, every colour except violet, some animals penned in a truck who know that something nasty's coming. A gathering, slow pilgrimage, and a chanting – it's like a flood of flotsam filling up the space, dust from biscuits past obscures the shack where it says 'Osram bulbs', another – 'Italian bikers welcome here', Singer and Hornby, Bauer skates – the life we promise, though it's all gone by from us long since.

Bella's entranced. 'Not an installation,' I tell her, but she says, 'Bigger than I've ever seen.'

She chants, 'More rituals, more rituals,' and who's to say she's wrong or right? My mind goes to

the raft, we're trashing up and down, and raising
dust and toxic mud, the houses all blown up, the
asphalt lakes in smoke, the trees – ah, the trees, a
tale of drought and shredding, no shade now for
goats and herdsmen, and should we weep with them
– the scientists escorted seem quite glum, but see
them later in the bars, they're dancing on the tables
with the rest and stealing stuff for souvenirs . . .

The raft, the raft!

I tell my friend, 'Apocalypse! Forgiveness
seems in order,' but he's indifferent, the bombing's
done some excavations, and the past's dug up,
exposed, and everyone is shipping marble home,
mosaic carpets for the patio, sickles and furnaces,
red satyrs on the go around the frieze in bathrooms,
spilling into rooms that serve for – what? 'Rituals, no
doubt,' says Bella, and no doubt she's right.

Hector the Boss feels out of place, 'Hey,' he says,
'These guys are rough – they don't react, they act,

the kind of power they want is not mine at all – I know the type, and I want out,' there's no one here to boss, because the plume count says it all.

'I'd solve it all by marrying,' he says, 'that Major now, she's quite the ordering kind,' but she's quite firm.

'I only marry ones above,' she says. 'Colonel's the minimum, this kind of pasty guy, the Boss, he's not for me, a lance-jack born, and busted down,' and Franco, dealer, has his way; they count the stores and make complicities.

He says, 'The Major's lost a lot of stuff,' and he can sell stuff fast, fast as it's flown in, but we go on escorting guys who've got some plan and if they can they don't come back, but make some bucks with tales as tall as they can tell them, long faces on TV and scaring presidents, and making others pleased that they're not here, but rather pay to make it go away – and we go on escorting guys, and losing stuff – but more is always flying in, a contrast with the raft where we are always throwing overboard, and Hani says it's just the dialectic kicking in, and smoke and dust and banging in the night with bombs and rockets, stuff that Franco's trying out.

'Impress the buyers,' Bella says, 'but let me fucking sleep.'

Paco, the politician, feels at home, he sheds his uniform, a splendid lizard he, though I'm not sure they shed their skins, but he's a find, a guarantee. The sects compete for him – Paco shows the world wherever he is courted that there is reason, moderation, all the things not wanted here, but there's a hope that when we go, he'll stay. We need his space, his kit is bartered, and for now, he has no gun.

I transfer my living to my truck. I tell Bella, 'Security, protection.'

'It's all protection, here,' she says. 'And security – I guess it's useful?'

'We'll need the truck to pack in all our friends,' I say, 'and all the stuff they've found.'

We've all become the Boss, the Dealer, while we're here – except for Bella. She's magnificent, blacker skin and violet robes, like Kali on her throne – a lotus: two tiny elephants with upraised trunks to water her.

'We'll finish here, then maybe go next door,' I say. 'There, everything is broken or run off, those stern rural guys, exporters – they've a good business, and we'll be paid the same.'

Bella looks closely at me: 'It's all protection, and security, you say it often, and it's all work for humanity, though for me – what holds me's all the colour here . . .'

'It's drab on drab,' I say.

'Aha,' she says, 'you're still not looking closely – shades of drab! the mosque-blue sky, then water, green and purple.'

'We've rather smashed it up.'

'It's all a composition, it will re-compose, turn into something new, the people here—'

'The people here loved funerals,' I say. 'Birth was precarious, life a pain, marriage essential, work

the same – only a death was final and secure, a
liberation if you like, passage that could be
celebrated, no looking back or forward . . .' These
people lived for death – more food for who
survived, shooting off your guns, real loss and real
emotion, even a solidarity, a sure thing.

I say, and she doesn't grasp it, 'Now we want to
bring a new precariousness, even power's uncertain,
one solid fate just melts away.'

'That's great,' Bella says, 'then we can be
together, all humankind, all with the same vision,'
and it's true, or maybe not.

I climb back in my truck and lock the doors and
try to sleep – a little shelf behind the seats. I never
learned to work reverse. I'll pack them in, the
Violets, with their loot, and go straight on –
security, protection! – till we find the plain, that's
green and watered, geese are running free, there are
no tents, just little shacks, no mines, no digging, and
no uniforms – and I laugh, and there is Bella, down
outside, I think I hear her say, 'You idiot.'

'Well,' I say, 'we found your colourful desert –

when do we leave and call it peace?'

'Effie will know,' Bella says, 'she's the one with low friends in high places,' and shortly, we pack them up, Hani and the rest, they sit demure on divans in the truck, the Major on the shelf. We choose a dawn when tides of Feasters clash with Fasters, I don't need to use reverse, the roads have been remade, although the towns are holed. There is one road, the Major has her map, but when we cross the border, here the road is stones. We leave the truck – we have alternatives, the artist-spy can't bring his Transam, but we have our mules – and on we ride, a-singing as we go, like pilgrims, and we've brought our shooting stuff and dynamite, and on with shouts and shooting, and – no regrets, the loot's abandoned – never was ours, so off with it – just take the cash, we hope it's good, besides, there's always more.

Only our good Doctor, Hani, is desolate. He thinks the raft's forgotten, but how could that be, with all these wrecks, these arks – stone ships – around?

I reassure him. 'Not protection, just survival,' I whisper, and he's cheered, but there's Bella, on ahead, she's far more plumes than I, a temporary general, no less, the bandsmen strike up Henze's Raft, but lurch around, and out comes Egk.

There is space here, unpenetrated, not a gram of junk, the compounds are walled round with mud, and mud inside, the animals seem much the same, and Bella shouts – 'Infinite gradations,' and we change our violet uniforms for peach, our plumes now golden, and we blend, but still bring peace, tranquillity, and lots of other stuff.

There is no one.

Dr Hani laughs, he says, 'And there you are! Or maybe aren't! You say "there is" and, simultaneously, "there is" no one,' and he chuckles, but I see there's just a blank page in his notebook, on the cover he's put 'communicative action', but there's no one here at all. There's dust, and things that might be structures fallen down, but no rags, no bones, it's desolation, and we find that we forgot to bring the food – the mules plod on, we couldn't think of butchering them, they are our only friends, though I could weep – my poor great truck we left behind – the Major didn't bring her map, and makes one up with coloured crayons.

'Major,' I say, 'you've put in towns and towers, markets and minarets, fair fields – maybe of soya, sunflowers tall as eucalyptus – but there's nothing here.'

She says, 'This desolation's only passing by, I'll map what was and what will be. Your presentism's just an error, illusion, lack of faith,' but we are suffering, Yusuf is drooping like a lily – the musicians improvise 'Three Oranges', but they left behind their keyboards, and the sound is thin, even the third orange turns out dry, and Yusuf says, 'Bring me the cook, I'm dying,' and we hush him.

We call for Hani, and he says, 'Not brains but consciousness,' and we shout that if that's all he's thought of after all those deaths and carrying stuff

and breaking it or stealing, then he's better off as
cook of mushrooms – then we find some in a cave,
poor withered things, and he's no pot or fire or
water, and we eat them raw.

9   Exploring

THE MAJOR'S map comes all alive! The mushrooms do their friendly work, the mules take off and sprint, they're like Transams, their hooves throw up the dust, it's turquoise, lapis lazuli and even sapphires, Bella's entranced, 'it was the sun that turned the violet into peach,' she sings like Effie and the sound expands like waves of sparkling water, and we grab the fish – they're pleased to be of use – the towns, the minarets on Major's maps arise, the road is made of marble, green and crimson – Yusuf is walking on his hands, the trombones bray in tune. Those are no helicopters, they must be flying asses, silk pavilions of notables and sages – here there is statuary, and the caves are full of manuscripts – and we read the poems and the riddles, recipes and prayers, and everything is in its place – and when the mushrooms end their trip, we find we've lost the mules, and all our guns and stuff, and we're once more alone. But Hani feels quite vindicated, and we're refreshed with toadstool wisdom and its insight, but he says, 'It's a delusion, you guys ate them raw. It's cooking gives them culture – now we've to plod on foot, and back to drab and thirst.'

But we have seen the light. Here there were armies, empty spaces, and such solitude – the guys that could, have left, the others wait and fear the worst – and now in fact we hear the worst, and far away there's dust arising, grey pommels – 'that's explosions', we all exclaim. And so, our way is clear.

We turn around, and after days and days of suffering, of thirst that brings poor Yusuf almost back into hallucination, but leaves him grey and speechless – we all, save Bella, feel a sadness. She sings like Effie, if there was anyone they'd sure have shot at us, but no, her voice expands, the plain is full of minestrone, hills of hot cheese, indeed a proper pizza ever stands before us, and the musicians throw away their gear, and join the song,

and on we travel, happy pilgrims singing lusty. We
didn't see a shrine, or realise our prayer, but as my
friend says, as he breaks his vow and speaks,
'There's nothing here for us. No fucking shrine or
anything.'

We find the truck, it's empty and been trashed,
but down that metalled road there's bread, and
maybe water too. We gallop like the mules we lost,
and spare a tear for them. Their destiny – who
knows!

The Major says, 'Now, you Violets, bags of
swank!' we shamble back – there's lots of people
here, the town is shattered but at least there's bread!

'It's always singing that wins wars,' says the Major.
'When you must go, then let it be a joyous sound, joy
signifies a victory, even though it's been a suicide.'
She packs the things that's left, and says, 'I'll just
deposit my map in the national library, if I can find it
– they must have moved the books.' She stares

around.

'Bella, you can be general, take all the plumes that suit you. And the rest,' she eyes the musicians, Yusuf with his hot dog, Hani haggling for a ladle – the Boss, the Dealer, and my friend – they're busy making contacts, and, I suppose, they punish enemies, their own, their friends' enemies, and just those who may not fit.

'The rest are honourably discharged,' and she whispers, 'though into what?'

'As for you,' she points at me. 'You're dishonourably everything.'

I'm amazed. 'Why so?'

'You dishonoured the leadership.'

'I didn't see any – and I drove the truck.'

'And lost it. Trashed. Besides, you never see the leadership until you've won.'

Maybe if the whole world lived in tented camps and fought for food-in-packs – I'd be appreciated. Though I don't think it's appreciation that I'm after, but maybe that's what Doctor Hani's cooking up.

The Major says, 'It's quite untrue we ate those

magic mushrooms, that we left our guns and stuff –
we were the liberators – and those guys are now
quite used to liberation, have to learn to do it for
themselves,' and she snarls at me, 'I hate your sly
wolf face, that "wisdom from above", uncommon
touch, confusion, doubting, call it as you will,' and I
protest:

'That big Mack – needs clean boots to drive it
well.' She turns away, disgrace is not a thing you
hide from easily, and the guys commiserate, and
wave their papers, Bella waves her plumes, she's
like a Chinese general in the opera, and they
improvise an anthem, but without their guns they
can't shoot off a grand finale, so we sidle off, the
honourable and the less, and wait for lifting to that
Sixties house, so full of hope and plotting – and we
wish at least that Effie could have seen us, done a
dance to sweeten off the memories, but maybe
another front has opened and she's once more
Salome to the troops, a head she carries in a pouch,
and dance and dance, and in the contracts come, the
veils come off, and it's once more the dancer not the

dance, but that is artistry, and she and Bella won all hearts.

We've to insert ourselves in new careers, quite improvised.

Bella says, 'I want you to produce my record. Effie will be mad.'

'Of course. That's how things go nowadays.'

Two generals have convoked us. Bella says, 'We're not army.'

The room is tiny, on the wall there's a plan of what it should contain, someone's drawn in two generals and facing them, two shapes.

The Generals are called Van Buren and Al Qatari. 'You can call us Van and Al.'

'We're not army,' Bella says again. 'We didn't find anyone to protect or liberate, and so we left.'

I see a newspaper – headline says, 'The Violets Shrink,' and Bella says again, 'We're not army,' and she adds, 'But I'm a general.'

They read out her record – it's a tale of coming out on top and doing down her friends. But I am not a friend. I ask, 'Why am I here?'

'If you don't know, you shouldn't come,' says Al, but Bella says, 'We all need protection, guys are out to get us, who knows why, it's all confused, the answers seem quite fabulous – unless it's just vainglory, wanting in, and jealousy, who can tell? And where will you two push it, what's the endgame? Will it stop when you've exhausted everything and everyone, and leave it to some other guys – or maybe it's religion here? That does seem quite unlikely! In any case, we stopped, there's dust and ruins – this guy here—' she points to me with some disdain '—he screwed it up, they trashed our truck, our cook without a pot or ladle . . .' and so, and on and on.

'I'm just a music guy,' I object, 'I love her voice,' but Al and Van are hotting up, it seems that Bella loves her plumes, will fight to save them, but I'm dishonoured and indifferent, it seems to me we'd all best start again, and live in tented camps and see if we like that, and maybe start a different way, like Dr Hani says, but Al dives in, with 'If you run, it makes it seem some game – fought out with lethal stuff,' and I interrupt and say, 'The mushrooms saved us, and the vision was so clear.'

Bella softens. 'You take it all so seriously, not knowing what it's all about, where it will end, and after, when it's ended, where it goes to.'

The generals retire.

'What's this about endgames?' I ask her. 'What do they know or care? They'll hammer along until someone else takes over, some country with another slant.'

'We're on the outs,' she says. 'Maybe because we lost those guns. Or didn't build a school – you didn't leave the blackboards in the truck?'

I think of Effie, her 'low friends in high places'.

I say, 'They want a percentage of your recording!'

Bella says, quite proudly, 'Entertainment for the forces – big and important, taps right into those big cubes of currency they ferry in,' and she shows her network, web that's made by spiders bigger than the ones I've known, more sticky, more resilient, and I say, 'I thought you were an ingénue.'

She laughs, 'That's been my strength. I study detail, that is all,' but I think of her, her voice, in that grey plain that even poor people found too tough, the voice that billowed out, a cloud of sentiment that filled the emptiness with emptiness – but feeling good and giving hope.

The generals return. 'We think,' says Al, 'this guy deserves the honour of his discharge – you, Bella, you should stay a while, a general that's searching for her honour,' and he smiles at Van, though neither of us is honourable, nor cares a spit what judgment's passed.

Van makes things clear. 'We're your agents now,' he says. But –

'There's nothing we can't do,' I say and after all, we have survived our tour with criminals and visionaries.

'You may not know it now,' Al declares, but you will find you need – protection.'

'If I need it,' I say, 'I've a raft!'

Van Buren says, 'That's maybe for escape, but not protection. That sister Effie takes it very bad, this sudden burst of singing, with new music spilling out.'

I ask, 'Do the generals want a song or a prophet?'

Bella says, 'I think – a singing prophet.'

'Effie won't love you for that. Will there be war between you?'

She's severe. 'You and this stuff about war – just because I'm doing deals with generals! Wars are a lubricant, they change everything, societies, all that. If you're attacked, what then? Or if you feel the need to stop some guy, some guys, that you don't like, ideas, all that?'

'I'm not a bigot, Bella, not a man of principle. Of course, these things will only work if they're made to work for everyone. I stand above the frays – don't start or stop them. What I think or wish, it doesn't change a thing. So, you're a general, into that mix you jump. But prophets have to prophesy, you must find a thing to say, you can't just hum along.'

'It's Al and Van. They've got the words.'

I say, 'You know, the propheting, the religion – that's only part of it, the froth, the mask, the alibi; it's armour, makes you look quite fierce, determined. What'll you do for all the rest?'

'Music!' she says, 'People all over hum along, the songs are glue, or honey, sweet and sticky. The other stuff, the dire, goes on, but you can be a cool and with-it gal or guy, a-singing, if they let you, even do a little dance at home – music's the thing, the modern thing.'

'They'll take your plumes.'

'Of course not – that's my costume.'

In the studio, Bella sounds like a frog in a bottle.

'What have I lost?' she wails. 'In no man's never land, I was a fury!'

Al is distraught. 'What message is all this?'

'I like your Allenby shorts,' I say, but he's not pacified. He and Van have interests – Van in the gyms that people need, Al in the drinks you have to take.

'What exactly is your army?' I ask. 'I'm confused.'

'The army of the good. Pacification, not bigotry – and with Bella here, we could mobilise the mass, do down the sects, and unify!'

'I hear Effie's got up an army of the bad,' I say, 'we shall have duels, coloratura at dawnbreak.'

'Everything is freezing up,' Al says. 'New powers, new riches, new – and old – the discontents. We're on the run, it's getting tough, this world re-ordered.'

I see the future as it lies in tented camps, or maybe rented rooms – but I've no voice in this, it's just distaste, or squeamishness, for horror and its makers – Maker, as they used to say. And there's a flaw in this, this vision. It's sentimental, ladles on the sugar. You can't say honey now the bees are dead. It's life! before us, on it roars, last train but then – tomorrow brings the first train, on we hop, we're off again! We'll have to clash our shields and hope we've got the ones with Gorgons' heads.

'Now, lots of poor are rich,' Al says, 'or nearly so, religion and tradition, all that stuff, give way to shopping in the malls: the army of the good . . . it's growing dark.'

He does look threatened, but here's Van, who's coaching Bella with the words. 'The trick lies in the rhymes,' he says, but then, 'I can't pronounce this rubbish,' Bella says, and we're a tableau here – musician guys with trumpets ready for a bray, and I who's paying them for silence; Al and Van, who see the masses in their gyms, all keen on life eternal or at least with muscle tone – they see the cash is leaking out. They say to me, 'The big idea! That's what we want,' and though I have one, I'm not sure I trust them with it.

The Major says, 'We Violets – never lost a person,

now, we should band together, help Bella find her voice. Wherever it may be,' and I think, If it is.

'I never heard a quest so trivial,' I say. 'When we trained, the programmes were severe. Remember – "Hostage without ransom, hostage with death". "Things or people put together after bomb". Ourselves – likewise. Remember – "Limbs glued on the wrong way round" . . .'

'Hard to forget that one,' says the Major. 'But that's all passed into the imaginary, that sort of cloud-shaped hat that doesn't reach your head. Now, it's the case that only artworks, songs and stuff, can carry messages – all the rest is spies and lies.'

Amid the chuckles and the frowns, I say, 'This band here is spies, for sure,' but she is rolling on.

'Bella rises from below,' she says, 'Effie's with the top guys.'

But Hani's on my side, he doesn't trust the tiny, nor the shading. 'Big is business, small's just small,' he says, and though we'll not say so, Effie has our hearts, she's got the contacts.

Top guys – love them, hate them – where does

she find them? Still, we're in the gang, we still wear bits of uniforms, our mission is to save mankind – at least, identify it – the trail is white, untrodden, darts ahead. We can't resist a quest.

'We wanted to be noble, but we turned out crass,' says Al.

'We hoped to be noble, but we was crass,' says Van.

'If we'd read the books,' Al goes on, 'we'd have known – it was no go. Rather, it was go and come back. We wanted to bring order and call it freedom, but we smashed what order there was, and brought no freedom.'

'In the mirror, we saw gods,' Van says. 'We turned round, and there were harpies.'

'And worse, much worse,' says Al, shaking his head.

'So,' I say, 'you've lost. Your empire's fading into books, historians. Now there's transition while we wait, it's "warring kingdoms", till another monster comes to eat up all the little ones. Better to be Bella, looking for garnets in the dust. Or Effie with her loud friends, who come with gifts.'

'Better to be someone,' says Al, mysteriously, and Van nods, says, 'So, we got into fitness,' and Al puts in, 'And fitness drinks.'

Fitness and drinks. All useful for the raft, the ship is going down, I think.

'What distresses me,' says Al, 'is that when I go, I won't have left a mark.'

'Surely, not leaving a mark is rather good,' I say.

'My drinks will finish down the toilet.'

'I've no words,' I say.

'The army promised more,' he says, and Van agrees.

It angers me. I say, 'Don't you see, it's coming down, it's crashing down? First you used money, with some fine words. Now, you must send your armies here and there, where they're not wanted, and they try impossible things, your money's running out, how long can you borrow it from guys that's doing better, and have no love for you?

'You've no place here, in the new world – you think you made it, but it made itself. You think you were the perfect model, the exceptional, you saw your faults, but not how deep. And who, in other countries, would live a life that someone else has lived? Leave no more marks, build no great wall. Keep keeping fit, until the end, and let the other guys go on and sort themselves. Order or freedom, now, it's not your call,' and my anger wilts, the words have lost their scent. Al, Van, they look at me, they want to understand.

'Yet you were a mercenary,' Van says, 'and on the army side.'

He has a point.

'The world is full of armies marching up and down,' I say, 'they all bring hospitals and suchlike – it's all the same,' and yet it's not, and Dr Hani has it right, we just need bigger brains, or else we have outlived our species' powers, and if there are a million years to wait, we'll spend them on the raft, a curiosity. But Yusuf, rising from the ashes, says, 'We'll never live another million years,' and ambles out, and at the last he says, 'That great stone ship's not sinking. It has sunk.'

'Hey, friend! Room up there on your high horse?' Al says nastily to me. 'Now you're in the music biz – lots of guys there are criminals, maybe – you too?'

Van says, 'Let the little fish alone – we knew it had to end, but not in tears. Resistance. We'll fight – that's been our trade.'

'Goddam it,' says Al, working up. 'The guys that served along with me – most every one is rich, and has an old Impala to fix up, pinball machine or two, a lovely wife, you can't have more than one, but that's the rule.'

'Calm, old pal,' Van says. 'This guy is just sub-agent to ourselves, a-selling Bella. We always knew it ends, the power, the civilisation too good for all

the guys that wanted in, or who were in and wanted
out. It always ends like that – you're doing well, and
then the emperor converts and over everything are
fucking Christians, then the Huns, you do your
deals, but all that's left is ruins and some buried
coins. The world wags that way, Al, and we shall
fight it to the end.'

But Al is firing on his eight and says, 'This guy
here, before us now, dishonoured patsy type, let's
start resisting him,' and I regret my praising of his
shorts, he's tried so hard, assimilate to who knows
what, and off we go, a quarrel at the start. Young
Yusuf goes back where he lives, inside his corpse,
that ruined envelope, and down he goes, wise man
waiting for leftovers Master Hani doesn't do.

Then, I see the map that Al and Van have drawn, it's
on the wall and huge. We are encircled, we are
civilisation.

'Look where they are,' says Al. 'Our foes, them

terror guys. And they're just forerunners, a bunch of cats and weasels, trained as infantry and armourers, the big guys haven't entered yet, they wait their game – those few guys, some bombs, some bullets, they have shook our lot,' and he goes on in fugue, 'The big guys, real big guys, they haven't entered yet, they're doing deals and buying cash and saying tut how terrible, and some are keeping quiet, the real big guys – look where we're sending guys and losing them, look at those shitholes where they go and there is nothing, just the usual poor and sick, the real big guys is waiting time,' and on he goes, and Van is nodding out the beats, and I remember Bella keeping time with pearls, like they were a rosary, and squinting down at little sharps and flats that look like insects getting in the jam – and there's an air of high finance and strategy, of chiefs, and chiefs of staff and pins and flags in maps, and maybe lady soldiers chalking up the loss of who was that? and shed a tear, and all.

Van turns to me. 'Now, where's your raft in all of this?' he says. 'Where you go to make your landfall, friend? Your girls, Bella, Effie, fighting like two squirrels, and all your funny crew . . .'

'They're not funny, just other things,' I say, but he's quite right, we're racing in between two storms – civilisation on the left is bowing out, and armed; the whole world on the right, exhausted and infertile, wilts like a dying lily, and I think: With luck, the raft just drifts, it's indecisive, exists just for survival, and I think some more: Remember, when they say that every human is of equal worth, so as we float along we must be worthy, and maybe we'll find a desert spot, no one to criticise or chronicle, and start again, where Dr Hani can pursue his studies, not injecting us, just help us make a paradise from trees and birds, the insects too, and mushrooms if there are.

'There's mushrooms almost anywhere,' I say aloud, but Al and Van don't get the link, talk only of their 'bunkering down', their 'deals to save the thrones and jewels', and Van says, 'books and stuff,' and Al agrees and hands round drinks.

'You want to lay off those mushrooms,' says Al. 'I ran into trouble there once.'

'Keep our powder dry,' Van says sternly, and I don't follow, think of them both stuffed with it, that powder, dust, decay, big bangs, and when I tell the sisters, Bella says, 'I don't see encirclement by foes.' Later she peers at their map, the eye of God that sees every little thing, but only little things, old-fashioned god, but quite meticulous.

'They've skewed this map,' she says, but I know it's in their minds.

'Who are the big guys, biding time out there?' Effie says. 'I'd like to meet them,' and she laughs, and will.

Dr Hani's solemn. 'Civilisation never really stops,' he says, 'it all depends, the idea of it or just the different guys a-doing different things and not quite understood,' and I think that not quite understanding means he's overdone the mushrooms, for I don't understand a thing at all, in any way – those people running from each other and us paid to make them stop and live in tents, the lucky ones – and here we come to luck, and that is not at all the rule. When making human sacrifice you really shouldn't choose by lot or luck, but by attractiveness or something so; the animals, well, there can licence be – I'd sure need take on a lot of mushroom juice, that's just to bear to watch the sacrificing – and Bella catches me, I'm sliding off, I'm sliding off the raft, she says,

'It's worth it all, those crested snakes in jade, with amber eyes, the singing, can't you hear it, that is civilisation, yes!' and it seems she's found her voice, though who knows what she'll sing, out just comes noise that floods around the world, catches some attention for a while.

'We call this the armoury because it's full of arms, but not the kind that fire,' says Van, crossly.

The rock it's carved from is wonderful – rocks of chalcedony, blue john, the green, the red, the streams of peat, sherry and port, claret and holy wine, the veined, the pure, some splintered from explosions, some rust-stained, some nailed and pinned, some swooping down like claws. Here lie the arms . . .

What fine machines – yes, the arms on slot machines, also threatening boxes, implements for torture, and for exercise, machines for cola drinks, others for coca, all the names memorial and traduced – the Dr Salt, the Mustard Fizz, the Ruby Sweet. And pinball games – some with the 'tilt' removed, to play forever, there the hooded heroes, there the bold-chested ladies, masked, astride their rockets. Al listlessly shoots a ball or two: gets his ping ping ping. The other Violets, bandsmen, sidemen, goggle at the marvels.

'I don't recognise myself in this, this civilisation,' I say, but I'm backing off, don't like being Mr Pompous.

'That's the beauty of civilisation,' Van says, 'not only does it go on forever – it's quite indifferent to you, your names, intentions, all that stuff. It's all mulched in, your Goya and your Delacroix, Pergolesi, Wagner – into the pit they go. They are all yours and no one's, for or against – in a thousand years they'll all sit battered in the same display case, the same video, side by side, scholars will come and speculate on what kind of guy you may have been. OK – it really isn't you – what do you care?' – and so and so.

We stand in silence. Bella's entranced, the rocks could hold her for a hundred years, and Effie's taking notes, Hani's found a corner where the fungus grows, and Yusuf's buying those brown and yellow drinks. The band has found a jukebox, here's the primal rock, the Comets are still arching through that ever-midnight sky, their pelvises are jigging, anomalous and not for sex, at least not yet – they're constellation warriors – just like Orion, rocketed up to joust and jangle over us . . .

'Time! now! enough!' says Al. 'We've shown you all our secret store. Resistance needs the Violets, you need to come on board . . .'

'You sure mean to have lots of prisoners,' I say,

cages and shackles, those tricky boards and wires for getting some intelligence stretch far away.

'We don't just shoot them,' Van says primly, 'We're the humane ones,' and he points to me. 'This guy was into humanity, but gave up. That's not the spirit – and besides, that raft of his – it's got no armament, it's decking, like your garden patio.'

I've never heard of fighting rafts, I think, they're for necessity, save your own skin – and otherwise it's war canoes, or those hulks that carry planes, but Bella's trilling in her throat, frog becomes princess, she waves her plumes – not just a singing, but an optimistic propheting.

'We've just to write the word,' says Al.

Effie tells us all, 'Wanting to survive is still something positive, it's not just panic. It's you – together with your baggage, your burden. The trouble is – you want to be the captain of your raft, and shipwrecks don't accommodate like that.'

'The captaincy's reserved,' I say. 'It's mine,' and how I wish I could leave them both on board the ship, Bella and Effie, as it sinks, – but Bella's a character in my life, and Effie – well, she'll tag along and plot and pout . . .

'But I won't drown!' she says.

It will go on, maybe in some form more horrible, there'll be a stretch when paradise – or at least perfection – has been reached, then it will fall apart again, the lessons faster, faster, piling in on one another, and we shall stifle underneath the pile. Someone, somewhere, will take it up and start again – next time universal currency and the global jail. Maybe we broke the mechanism, eternal regeneration – needn't always be, not onward, upward, any more, but slither down and down, no getting up, the face is unrecognisable in the glass, the water. No longer young and maybe beautiful, but burned and shrivelled. So: scramble on the raft, which goes where nature wants it. Well, I'll command the crew, but not the waves.

Al says, 'The band will be assault troops.'

'Rubbish,' I say, 'they're session musicians, not drawn towards suicide. One gig at a time, a day, their creed,' but Van is firm,

'There's no more work, it's all on line, live guys are just a drag. Call it security, call it humanity – it's all to save some healthy bodies, drive off the others. It's a battle, Chief,' and he hits me, quite hard, on the body, as if to see if I've got armour, or will resist.

'Defeatist,' Al snaps at me.

'Now everyone's a target,' I think. Once, it was archdukes and the like – you snuffed the flame, and darkness came. Now, a few guys, anonymous, with actions picayune, clever and sly – and in the long term, trivial, inflated aims, the unattainable – can rock the tower, whole structure of philosophy and the everyday. Is it so precious? Our burrow, habitat? Well, we can't belong elsewhere, so – down with the ships you go! Down with the world.

But the raft, the raft of the Medusa, what does that, its castaways, represent? Escape, survival, suffering. Abandonment. And rescue! Who's to rescue us? Those were fine days, when rafts were sighted, saved. We have no other home, we don't belong, save on the raft. No hope of rescue. But we'll not sail with Van, nor Al.

I see them marching now, in boyscout shorts, then there is Bella, like a quinquereme, singing her anthem, and the guys, the Violets, plodding along behind, each step a hop to keep in step, they count in two's, and Bella's free and beatless, unarmed but not pacific, thinking of all the riffs unplayed.

'You underestimate my top-guy friends!' Effie says. 'They'll lead us on, and even make us safe.'

I guess who she's teamed with, say, 'Hector and Franco, boss and dealer, they're just street dirt.'

'Hector the investor, Franco – where do you think Al and Van got their arms?'

'You're very well informed,' I say.

'You go abroad, you'll find they have respect. Here, they just use their little telephones, and walk

around, just like talking to themselves, but there—'
and she waves a cosmopolitan paw, 'You see a hole,
before you in the sand. You clamber down,' and I
see Bella's plumes that disappear into this
wonderland, 'And there's the pavilion, clad in
watered silk, the fittings made of brass and gold,'
and I think, Allenby's treasure and his armaments,
and she goes on, 'and aviaries and plates from
Isfahan, and carpets from Shiraz,' and I think, Poor
stuff, and vulgar, and she says, 'The desk is pearl,
with furnishings of jade that's white as polar bears,'
and on she goes.

I see Hector and Franco, sipping their juleps,
filling in the orders while sweaty guys load up the
trucks, and I say, 'It's a picture of gritty people
circulating grit,'

She's offended. 'Well, my boy,' she says,
'that's how it works, that's how you get respect. Not
by killing friends. You have it circulate, and every
time a circle is complete, you find it's grown a little
tuft of bucks or similar, and you shave it off,' and
she looks at me dreamily, 'And put it in your safe.'

'Where does Bella fit in?' I ask.

'She designed it all. It's Hector's refuge!'

How I wish I didn't have them on the raft, and needn't tell the bandsmen not to hoard up pets, it's not an ark, but for emergencies, no goddam animals to upset the trim, and they just laugh, they've got a bunch of things that sting, in bottles, things that smell, in wicker baskets, things that kind of sing in caskets, and it falls away, the big idea, and Franco buys and sells, the stuff goes round and round and rusts away and Hector takes his cut.

Well, I'll talk to them. I say, 'Call me Captain – I'm not captain of anything, yet. Just – not an army rank – a name.'

Hector says, 'Saving civilisation – it does you credit.'

'I couldn't care less,' I say, 'it's just transition, when the new tough guys take over, or when we fizzle to extinction.'

'Well, we're all alongside you,' he says, and I think, just mind my paint – approach but do not touch. That's what relationships are, can't put to sea without some lifeboats. Put your relations in a ship, relation-ship comes out – a bit it's unavoidable, sometimes it stirs you – all those ships becalmed, like folded wings of white doves, headdresses of nuns a-floating through their tasks. Like tents becalmed, starting again, all the discontents . . .

10   Smara

P ACO HAS an answer, a solution. 'Move them
all around. Stick minority to minority – then
you will find a small majority! Encircled,
it's true, but quite quite large. Each for his own –
split and join. Move them from the mountain to the
plain, from estuary to desert. Homogeneous, tribes
with all the customs shared.'

'Where is the hole, the hole that Hector built?' I
ask.

'It's near Smara,' Effie says, 'he keeps old
names – nearby the desert that's called Ga'a.'

'We travailed through all Africa, but Bella
never said she'd been to Smara.'

'That's her business,' Effie says, and I think,
'So, Bella's been behind it all, but what and why?' –
and Effie says, 'Hector was once lithe and snakey,
holes in the desert were his thing, all kinds of trade,
salt . . .' and she fades into silence.

'Then he plumped up, turned whiter?' I prime her.

'He teamed up with Franco, they became a corporation, from low places, they moved up – to high friends, high windows overlooking parks. Arms. And legs. The arms to shoot with and the legs to carry all that stuff.'

'Are you convinced it's coming to an end?' Dr Hani asks. 'Talking of ends, that threat to kill your friend! – a kind of mutiny, a darker ship indeed, no ports for that one – you only had to give the people shelter, didn't have to love or like them. If it all goes down,' and he waves at the pot, his stock, the chanterelles a-simmering, jars of dried and moist, under oil and under salt, and under vinegar and under peppers, under who knows what, 'All this, my civilisation . . .' and he stares, desperately.

'I am convinced,' I say, 'and there's an end. Maybe I'm also wrong, and – nothing will end, there is no time abstracted, just duration, it's only us that grow restless in the pauses, fearful in the mudslides, all that stuff that comes into your room when you're asleep. And revolutions – that we long for, yet, when they come, they often bite us,' and he nods, abstracted.

'Your cooking will endure, my friend,' I go on. 'Music and idols – they may not, and sex will go, but cooking, like the wheel, the broken horse, goes on. I'm not so sure,' and I peer out at the Facility, where every month or so there is a sheet of T, of truth, that tells – not us – of what is really going on, of where the figures lead, and who is planning what – 'Not so sure your philosophy survives.'

He gestures with his ladle. 'I'll cook up something, then maybe I'll toss it out, or fill the bin – that's what mere stew is for. Its essence can't be rendered down,' and I think of Bella, Effie, busy with their qualities, the voice, the eye – nothing can damage those, though what it is that Bella does, for whom, and what she knows, and why she brought me down, I can't conceive.

'Bella feels – you should love the people more,' Hani says, 'or should have. When it all comes down, it's down, but meanwhile—'

'Maybe it was just enough to do my tasks, not do that species questioning.'

'These little chaps are ready,' the good Doctor says, and I drink his broth. It turns me inside out, a rubber bottle or an architecture that's painted on the sky, these low flat palaces of mud, you light the stars, the constellations, half a twist to left or right, and all's powered up, the forest canopy is red and green below, birds hop around your knees and far above the steel blue masts support some scrambling beasts, monkeys perhaps, but surely not, they carry rifles and they're shooting, firing down, and Hani pops up into frame and says, 'Sorry, my friend! – that trip's for someone else.'

'I'm not a crook, you know,' Hector says, 'just got bad friends, and once the habit takes you . . . worst of all is Franco, for he plans. I execute,' he laughs. 'Or rather, once it was me that did the tawdry stuff, the discipline, and Franco was the judge, the lawyer. I execute, he plans, and then it's me who's executed,' and he chuckles at his joke.

'How come you built that hole in Smara?' I ask.

'It once seemed safe, but now, alas, the fittings are all sanded up, maybe the hole is blocked – the price of Bella's work will rise.' He looks sad.

I press him. 'Did she specialise in holes, all fitted out for business?'

'We used to say she was the eye of God, but now,' he says, dismissively, 'she's just intelligent design,' and again he laughs.

'She's quite vindictive,' I say.

He nods. 'She brings a justice to the little things, the things that creep and question.'

'End of the world – it's a big thing – anyone can make an error about that.'

'Ah yes, but in the meantime...' just like Dr Hani.

I hear them shouting in the next room, above the bubbling of the pots and the trilling of Bella.

'The Captain,' she says. 'After storming heaven – the shebeen – he's into holes in the desert.'

'He's sure that everything will close right down,' Hani says. 'And there's an end to it.' He means it, though he has his doubts.

'Wants the Medusa – us – to sink, then he's Noah on his raft!' Hani says.

'He's the one who wants to close it down. I have a message, with the truth. Messenger of Death, that's what he is. That raft will never float, never find a landfall – it is extinction, Bella.'

I imagine them staring at each other.

'I've got my prophecies,' Bella says, 'my war with Effie, who's the biggest diva – what else should wars be all about? We're civilised – it should be songs, and not the singer.'

There is silence, then Hani says, 'There's work and cash with Al and Van. If the Captain is angelic, he should see we need them – for us, it's all in meantime, in the waiting. Who gives a fuck if it will happen, end and nothing – pouf! It's what we do meanwhile, and he should realise, he's not the man of destiny – it's chance! Here there's a mudslide, there a genocide, – you do not take your pick, you take your luck.'

'That's good sense, good Doctor,' Bella says.

'Of course,' Hani adds, 'dishonourable discharge is quite his codename. That is he! That is his ID!'

We each have our cop. Mine says, 'For every bullet, every bad intent – a corpse. I'm watching and I'm counting, and I'll follow you.'

'I'm innocent,' I say, 'you'll waste your time.'

He laughs. 'You get your innocence when we've proved your guilt and made you pay – whether the desert, or in China, I shall be your shadow – you, your own phantom,' and he makes the sign, sign of the third eye that knows before it sees. I nearly give the finger, but remember – that way they remember you, so doff the hat I haven't got, and leave.

Cops are for punishment, detectives are for justice – for me, no justice, just pursuit. No cadavers, so no end. Everyone, somewhere, survives. Me – abandoned and abandoning . . . Always in command.

'Pitiful,' says Bella.

'I can't get rid of you, it seems,' I say to her. 'Where there's hate there's love, they alternate but also pull together, like two mules in harness.'

'You should try my sister,' she says.

'You're at war.'

'Only with our vocal chords,' she says. 'Besides, she's always room for footmen in her court – I travel light, and near the ground.'

'I'll forget that you denounced me,' I say.

'That job – you hated it.'

'A gentleman's objection, nothing more – a

philosophical malaise.'

'You made it seem quite drastic,' she says.

Again it's Hector, 'I should like,' he says, 'to go to China. Lots of business there. It's that, or back into my hole, back to Smara, with my jade and pearls.'

We argue as we fly across the sea. I'm the Captain, so should have jurisdiction over water, Van says no, command's of the personnel, not the terrain, and Al says he should be general on the sand. Below we see the craft, that's not quite ships and not quite rafts – the flotsam of the world, escaping, floundering and foundering.

'They've had their disaster,' Van says, 'made by us or gods, spirits of mountains, rivers, earth – or war, that every Prince should be prepared for, the sole, and the rewarding, study of his fight to stay afloat and maybe loved. Now . . .' and as he speaks, we see the craft below, they're plunging towards more disaster – some sailors fall in waves, are newly ghosts that cling to keels and pull their comrades down. Others will land and live out prison lives, at work or languishing.

'Our new citizens, that will transform the world,' Al says of these.

The plane's the comforting kind, can't fly too high, the engines sound like model Ts. We had to take our shoes off, like it was a mosque, and I remember how Mahomed used a flying ass for transport.

'I'm glad security is tight,' Effie says.

We see the arms and stuff are loaded through another door, and we all laugh, and when we land our cargo tinkles like a chandelier

'I hope we loaded food,' Bellaa says.

Dr Hani looks disturbed and Yusuf rolls his eyes, and here we are – a little band of tourists, or it could be warriors, explorers, priests of some new cult, or burned-out writers looking for a cheap hotel and servants, and it's hot as hell.

'I wish we'd gone to China,' Hector says. The artist-bomber sketches flat horizons, squared-off shells of buildings two metres high or less, and Hector says, 'Why don't you put some camels in,' the artist sneers, he has integrity, and anyway – here it's all junk, of plastic, stuff all inedible.

'Here in the desert, you should look for holes,' Bella says, 'like Hector's hideaway, beneath this lot there's clubs and caverns,' and we hear a roar, it's Van.

'March forward,' he says, but it's like marching back, there is no feature, and we stumble on.

'The desert stands for purity and contemplation,' Hani says, view of the sky, no earthly things to be corrupting, distract us from our inner quest,' and Yusuf says he's thirsty and we stare at him – there's nothing here.

We are scattered about, on a dune.

'Should we think of joining humankind, during this meantime?' I say to Bella.

'I'm in this war,' she says, brusquely, 'war with

my sister, you know.'

'But it's not like you,' I say, 'you are the queen of the minima, surfaces, lunar rocks, spores, lichens. Why do you want to be the last trump?'

'I'm quite competitive.'

'I know, I've experienced it,' I say.

In the plain, the artist, Mr Terrorart, is sketching – whether for fun or ransom, bring down the bombs, some kind of soft control – who knows. Then, we see from those low green-grey oblongs, windowless and doorless, people running, spilling out. They're like those stick-and-blob figures on cave walls – and we hear a humming, shouting far away, they're waving tiny shafts, so far away – they could be footballers, or fans, escaping, punishing, good time, bad time. And the artist sketches on.

At last he sees a threat in those approaching, slowly turns and walks away and runs and scampers, then he waves his arms, we hear a scream – 'Oh help me. Friends, oh help me' – and we stand and stare, and Al and Van are peering, we can't read the logic of the scene, hope some detail makes the story clear.

They're chasing him – but why? They can't have known he brings the bombs, maybe he's pried into their essence or their poverty, maybe he looks like someone else. They're bound to catch him, if we don't react. We don't react, though Al says, 'faster, faster', but the guy is going like a piston, and he's losing.

When he's caught, the logic is quite clear – the little band of creatures, blobs and strings, like ants – like ants they're bearing straws that must be clubs and swords – now he goes down, the little knot of arms and legs is in a spasm, then the antlike justices stand straight and make a ring and dance around, they sing and stamp, it's like a tiny bird burst from its egg, a chirp of wonder and success – something's fulfilled, and Bella says, 'Well! I never knew it could be over quick like that,' and Effie's got a telephone and sticks it in her ear, and who knows who and why she's called.

We turn away, we didn't like the guy, although we saw his talent, and it's clear that even in the desert there are lines – we've seen the frontiers, some are just on maps, and some ravines with mines, or walls and fences, some with cops who've to be paid, and some with desolation . . . Who would want to go from here to there, except quite casually? Van sends out a group of guys, musicians, bandsmen, and they ask, 'What's to be played?'

'Just bring back what you can carry,' Van says quietly. 'Scrape it off the sand.'

It seems he's quite a fine sand-general, a better one than Al, who's fussing with his clothes, and what they bring back is quite like roadkill, but so small! I wonder if they left some, but they have his sketching pad, the sand is crimson on his page, the little blocks – of dwellings, or of fortresses – are bright in black, like matchboxes laid down.

'We'll have to get it framed,' Bella says, but no-one wants it on their walls – we none of us has walls – or send it to his family – and what can they do with it, if they exist, and so we fold the paper up, quite carefully, and lay it down beside a rock, and we pass on, and in a while begin to sing.

'This is how he'd have wanted it,' Bella says, and no one says she's right or wrong.

Here's my friend, sidling up. 'The death sentence is suspended – for you,' I say.

'We've just seen one carried out. As justified as mine would be.'

'You let those guys into our camp, and they disgraced themselves. And us. Was it for revenge or for reward?

'Humane calculation,' he says, 'a little evil to avoid a greater. And your objection – doesn't seem like you.'

'Just reason, not experience.'

'Reason and experience lead to the same conclusion,' he says.

'For once, maybe.'

'Once is enough.'

'Enough for the guys we'd put into our tents,' I say. 'Our job, our only job, to keep them safe, then

– back into the millstream. We – you – failed.'

'You didn't risk.'

'I risked in everything.' That silences him

I'm not off my hook. I ask, 'Van, Al – their plan – is it security, something, that we're checking out – or drinks and gyms?'

My friend says, 'Our mandate doesn't make distinctions of that kind – "to bring peace, order, prosperity, check out the corrupt, fix the elections, sell your goods, do down the bad guys, and assist the good".'

It certainly covers bracing drinks – and football.

Hector's delighted, we're off to China.

The best this other continent, this Africa, could offer – apart from Bella, Effie too – was footballers, they were the best, but not hi-tech, those stadia, royal boxes all in gold and purple, the guys all fed with beef, new clothes they had, and how they kicked the ball! And not in anger, but in joy and pride – it made you weep to see.

'China, you'll regret it,' I say to Hector.

'The good thing,' he says, 'is – already they've forgotten why they had it, that revolution. Now they forge ahead, to be like us, but better, stronger—'

'Their menu stays the same,' Hani interrupts.

Hector presses on. 'This little band of ours – the music guys, they are our vegetables, but you, Captain, are the exotic tamarind. Bella's a sauce of sweetly sour. Effie is our peacock, done in butter from wild asses, or maybe Bella is the wondrous pomegranate, each gob of flesh as hard as ruby. I – well,' and he giggles in self-congratulation, 'a life of dedication to the fungi – a stew of stalks; and Yusuf's your bread roll, your stomach-stuffing,' and here, he smirks with disdain, and I think, no wonder Hani cooks the stuff and never makes a meal, and we are goddam hungry, but at least there's Franco, finding crates of booze, and we're all high, and play at switchback in the dunes – one of those vanished armies left their shields, engraved with Gorgon's heads – and we're not turned to stone or anything, just yelping up and down on sleds, till Hector lifts us off, away, and we meet Colonel Feng, who'll show us round security.

11 China

THE MAJOR says, 'It's not real rank, the Colonel's, he's got no men to boss around.'

'Those other revolutionary guys,' Hector says, 'the generals that made the deserts, or just conquered them – they thought too much about the past, those kings and queens and stuff, and then it all went wrong, and guys like us, Franco and our men, we had to take it over, just to have the area limping on,' and on he goes, Africa, China, all the rest, and Colonel Feng is bored but seems quite used to sleeping on his feet while other guys rant on.

There's uniforms around, and guys inside them – we don't know what they think or do, but we imagine it – those guys with order on their minds, but Colonel Feng says it's not just order, but also helping out, and Hector nods, we see the stuff they've got, in malls – and all the traffic, and it's just like home but all quite new and falling down already. Wow, can they shop! – and here's the banks to help them, and we stare at all the stuff they eat, those little stalls, it's like a veterinarian's specimen case, we turn away at first, but then – a length of snake, and little legs, and eyes like barley-sugars boiled in Chardonay – we scoff it down, though we don't chew, at last we eat and belch and everyone applauds, though Colonel Feng is hurrying us along, and hopes we'll do some trade.

Bella's into Peking opera, she screeches with her mouth tight shut and in a hundred years she'll maybe be accepted, but it's Effie who's a-signing deals.

'They're wise to pull the old stuff down,' Hector says. 'Forget, forget's the trick.'

'It's all the same as ours,' Franco says, 'but maybe better,' and we rush on from little stall to little stall, and eat and eat.

We do little justice to China. We marvel at the Wall, the prescience of keeping people in and out.

'It was to keep the barbarians in their place,' Colonel Feng says. 'Not needed now – we're the

barbarians,' and he laughs, and we laugh too, good
Colonel Feng, our friend.

We stroll around for weeks, eating curious things.

We meet people of all sizes, of similar beliefs
and aims.

'Yes,' says Hani, 'this is how it will all start up
again.'

It's hard to say if he is pleased – he'll have to
start cosmology all over, and his kitchen – what a
tragedy! Those skills outmoded, and, at last, Colonel
Feng asks, 'What exactly are you people doing here?
I don't see taking notes, or even much attention.'

'It's all the uniforms and such,' Bella says, 'and
police, the secrets, shapes and sizes.'

'That not at all what I am doing here,' Al says at
once. 'I'm keen on fitness, bodies perfect or at least
not gross.'

Van agrees, and says we dumped out military
stuff before we entered, and the Colonel seems

193

disturbed.

'I don't know what the others want,' Effie says. 'I'm always interested in more work – show me a stage,' and she trills a bit.

'And you?' asks Feng.

'Well,' I start slowly, 'I have in mind to understand whether our species starts again, and if it's so, according to your revolutionary principles...' though I've not convinced myself.

Feng's impatient. 'Yes, yes, I know all about that,' he says, 'but we don't talk about it now.'

'The Western empire's sinking now,' I go on. 'Civilisation's spread all round, it's just the same – and then we have this other fate, the planet's all screwed up, our species is endangered, should we just let it go – although, we have a stake . . . Then there's the raft, we watch the grand Medusa going down – the storms, the waves, no water you can drink, nor air to breathe – the ship, you understand, is just not viable. A metaphor, you see, stands as you wish – for planet, or for just the Western empire. At any rate, down it all goes, and I'm the captain of the

raft. A kind of prophet, if you like,' and think, On
the raft. Looking back. All turned to stone.

It seems extreme, and so I add, 'I have a cop,
he's waiting for the sums, the corpses, I'm
responsible for, and when he's proved my guilt, I
shall be innocent again,' and now it just remains for
Franco, and for Hector, they both spin their tale, and
so it's clear that for a while we'll go to jail, and so it
seems to go.

Yusuf saves us.

It would have been a long experience, jail, trials
and such. He touches Colonel Feng – just on the
arm, a gesture we would not have made.
Afterwards, the Major says, 'Not a gesture for a
military man,' but Feng is moved, and Yusuf says,
'Forget the explanations that the others make. We're
food tourists – what a wonderful country you have
here!'

It is a winning formula, everyone's relieved, we
scuttle out, and Al and Van have made their plans
for universal muscle tone, and that is all we'll ever
see or know of China.

'That was a small epiphany,' Effie says. She's angry, she'll not sing her arias there, and when we count ourselves, we find that Franco isn't with us.

'That crook has met his match,' the Major says.

I fear it's true, and Hector is contrite. 'I'm off back down my hole,' he says, resigned, 'the action here's too quick and scaring – poor old Franco meddled in . . .'

He doesn't finish but I'm sure it's held against my account, my cop is counting bodies and the missing, and my day will come.

We fly somewhere, the cash is running out – the surfaces of Earth are smooth, we're here and there and nowhere in particular, to go back home implies we have a hole like Hector, but I think of Hani's place, the building opposite, Facility, that turns out Truth, it's all quite dire, and none of us has any wish to start again.

Hani says, 'My life's work seems quite trivial,' the musicians take their Violets' uniforms and cut them up to make new clothes, the military life is past, we cannot win or lose, and money's really short, but Bella kisses me, just once.

'Captain, my dear,' she says, 'every grand ship is called *Medusa*, and they all go down, the people on the raft look back, and they are turned to stone,' and in a way that's consolation, though for her the stone or paint or any shiny surface is the same, and beautiful.

We go back to our Sixties house – we've nowhere else.

Dr Hani says that evolution's had its day, he places Yusuf on his guard, watching the Facility, to give alarms when messages – those with a 'T' – arrive.

'How can you tell at this distance?' I ask.

'That Yusuf is a genius,' Hani says. 'He got us safe and sound – except for Franco, that is true – out of that new empire, full of poor but maybe noble people, like they always are,' and he makes a sign to placate demons, or it may be spies: 'The guys in there, when "T" arrives, they wave their arms and whoop.'

'What's it for?' asks Yusuf, but we don't reply, he's just our holy fool, there is no discourse, and we know the only thing to do with 'T' is make a bet on it and hope it wins some cash.

Bella cuts a disc, her voice coaxed out, although the sound's already on the console, and the band's a base – they bring their instruments and sit around, and some smoke cheap cigars, and Bella, or some voice, sings a song, called 'She's a Prophet'.

She is famous, and the guys are pleased, especially as their instruments don't weigh as much as that old army stuff, but all the same the song just says that she's a prophet, and there's no sign of what she's prophesying, nor of what we mustn't do.

'Is that really mine? that ringing voice?' she asks, not waiting for replies, although it sounds like little dogs a-barking down a funnel, but she's pleased, but doesn't make a buck, the music and the fans are all somewhere in technoland, and so that's fame.

'Eternal art is done and dead,' Effie says. She's nestling up to some politico – and only then we realise . . .

'Paco! He wasn't with us when we left,' says Hani, and I must count him in, along with Franco, and the artist who can't now call in the bombs, those guys with lanterns on their heads who shoot up peoples . . .

'Maybe Paco's gone to supervise that installation,' Bella says, 'that big Wall they built, and painted green and ochre, brings the tourists in,' and I say maybe that's so, although they didn't need too many guys like Paco, having some millions themselves and knowing how to speak the languages, and Franco too – well, he's no great loss, and we have no responsibility.

The Major calls, I tell her of the missing and she says, 'It's not my job to do a body count – you must watch out for yourselves – I try to save your lives, if you drift off or lift your heads, that's not my business, if it's anyone's at all,' and off she goes, the musicians give the finger as she leaves, the military life is gone, and if there's war they won't be called, though they will suffer nonetheless.

Coda

ELLA tells me, 'I've a commission. Down the hole,' for Hector's called, wants new designs – the office, refuge, that he says he doesn't use for crime.

Hani is pleased. 'You send me salt – it's on a route,' he says, 'and I can send you mushroom soup, it's part of global interchange,' and so we go, Bella and I, part enemies, part lovers when there's need, part relatives, and part just joined by destiny or laziness. Desert of Ga'a.

'I have a plan,' she says. 'That desk of pearl – I'll make it stainless steel, the walls I'll make of fur,' and we get guys to kill a thousand little creeping things that squeak and squeal, maybe the last on earth, but they're not missed, there's no one here that misses them.

The telephone is old, brown bakelite – 'That's very rare,' says Bella, and '"Green malachite" the floor,' some gold and rosy *putti* hang above, and finish off the scene.

All the material's carried in by guys on camels, usually they bring the mail, and when they've done, they kill the beasts and buy a truck.

I wander off, the frontier's not so far, and parts are walls and parts are wire and parts have guards that wear those Allenby shorts – it brings to mind the gyms that Al and Van are bringing in, resistance as they call it, they've put one here, but no one comes, and sometimes for nostalgia I watch the tented camps, and then the guys without a tent, and then the guys that's running to escape, and other guys that's after them, and – paradise or cataclysm, both seem slow to come and Bella says, 'Content yourself,' and laughs as if she's made a pun.

Hector sits at his desk, pasty and plump.

'I'm straight in every way,' he tells us, and he's in contact with my cop. 'That tells you – I'm an honest man,' but we don't trust him, as cash flows in and we're not paid.

'The Captain's now two down and four to go,' he says – he means corpses, and adds, 'And we can't find your friend.' My friend. Three dead or missing, that leaves three to come, total six bullets from that goddam gun . . .

I even weep a bit. My friend! My enemy! Part of an earlier life – and every day we worship some old god we've found anew, and laugh a little, and put garlands in our hair, or paint our hands, or bray like asses in the dark, whatever those old scripts suggest, it's all a part of multiculture – the nursery tales are horrible all round, so too the quests, the tricks the gods get up to, and it keeps us sane, but it's too bad about my friend, although we know our friends all disappear one day.

Bella says, 'My next project is the raft – we've rather given up on humanity, new empires come, we've seen the start in China, although here there's no one yet, we're just a hole, with frightened guys that run around, and some with guns but they don't shoot down here, not yet, not in our hole.'

When I hear her good and common sense, I think, So, Bella, who probably I love, but do not like, just like real family, and yet . . . a pair of arms and legs to cuddle with.

Though it is cold at night, by day the hole is hot as hell, she didn't put the cooling or the heating in, it's no surprise – no power – I call to her, she's trilling like the birds we don't have here, not even vultures, here nothing dies, and if it did, I'm sure it goes on my account.

'Bella, what is lunch today?' I call to her, quite civilised, sophisticated, as if the good Doctor were at hand.

'Camel stew and mushrooms,' she shouts back. 'What did you expect?'

She has designed the raft. 'The sea will come to us,' she says.

We'll start to build. Maybe the others – the generals, musicians, singer, cooks and spies, my friend, – if he's been found – will come to us. Shall we escape the end? Maybe new empire's due to come? Or will it be destruction of our species, habitat – before we've found the key, new evolution that will let us breathe?

No oxygen, no water – or live in boiling sterile seas.

'Come on!' says Bella. 'New stuff's delivered every day, and I've dug up another vanished army, underneath the sand they left some marvellous stuff, and this will be the finest raft that ever finds no landfall, saves no humanity, presents a picture of survival to some painter guy that's waiting by no shore to capture us, that image of despair, or rescue, who can tell . . .'

Hani has sent – a kidney shape. It's bound in chrome – a leopard-spotted plastic floor, with little purple love-lights twingling round.

The Doctor sends a note – 'I found it in a club, a Sixties club, when life was easy, and the music wavered on till dawn, we drank, we fucked, and in between – we danced on floors like these. Take it, it's free, the basis of your raft,' and it's a treat.

'But it wouldn't float,' I say to Bella, and she has garlands in her hair – I think, but do not say, they look like snakes, but maybe we're just steeped too far in culture, civilisation, all that stuff, and all is portent.

'Have faith, dear Captain,' she says, 'look! I've found some golden thrones.'

Indeed she has, they're even of the hydraulic kind, up and down, balance of power, the emperor and his friend, and maybe patron saint or god, or guest, though now they're dry inside. And here are shields, nickel with cat's eyes, diamonds *en cabochon* – they must have been the guards' – and silver swords, and tiny altars for the field, and stuff that seems for dressing up, or maybe loot, it's quite a gaudy show – if you had paid to see the piles of stuff for war, religion and for having fun, you'd say 'it's finely made' as you pass on and through.

'We stack all this upon the raft?' I say.

'Have faith,' Bella says, and here are painted statues, precious too, more beautiful than all our friends, and well-proportioned, so she sets them up, it is a noble court.

'This is something of exquisite make,' I say.

'It's made before the gods were shuffled into that one powerful, ascetic, goodie bore we know today,' she says.

I agree, but say, 'It's all irrelevant to floating off, making good deaths or even founding something new,' but she's entranced, I hope she doesn't hope to make a show, and have the tourists swarming round.

'We'd better bury this,' Hector says. 'Those goddam snoopers in the sky, they'll see the glint and sparkle – down below it goes!'

'Maybe they won't all come,' says Bella. 'Your friend may not, for one. The living, yes, and those in flight. The dead have disappeared. Yusuf won't come, there's not enough to eat, and Hani has his other plan, not that it's much cop – and saying that, your cop will stay behind to make his count. Then, in a million years, if it's the fire and air, not earth and water, does for them – there they'll be: petrified, just like Pompei, undignified – just rocks. While we sail on.'

When they sense it's time, comrades will come and join us, leaving that house, the safe, safe house, where Dr Hani guarantees the calm, and keeps his eye on Truth.

'We'll have to fight them off,' Bella says. 'Or they could be a little private army, like they were in that dry place, where there was nothing, no one ran up to do us harm or greet us.'

'Humanity – it's all security,' I put in. 'Being military was just another way.'

She laughs. 'You know that isn't so – you want to make the people, the disastered ones, be good, or better, not just patch them up.'

'I'm not so stupid. I just felt, I feel, I've always felt – I'm on the wrong side.'

'It's the only side that will have us,' she says.

'Besides, it's all security.'

'Not mine, not my side! Maybe even I don't have one.'

'Humanity's made up of sides,' she says, as if she's wise.

'Everyone wants a bit of love, that's true,' I say, although it doesn't follow – neither by reason nor experience.

'Or a camel,' she says, 'they're more useful.'

'Look what an end they make!'

But they're still useful.

'Hector insists,' she says, 'must have a throne to sit on, on the raft.'

'It's not appropriate,' I say. 'I'm sure the whole setup's presided over by goddesses of war.'

'All the Medusa ships have goddesses.'

I go on, 'That Hector's an unworthy guy.'

She laughs. 'How you insist! You surely see that he's our boss, he'll sit there while you steer, or do whatever captains do,' and then I feel the life go out, it's not adventure any more.

'And will it all come crashing down?' I ask. 'Or

just go on, with guys that look like us, not better ones, but those who've got that installation, the Great Wall that doesn't serve, except to bring the tourists in.'

'Tourism's the lubricant,' Bella says, 'and it saved us, thanks to Yusuf.'

We ponder for a while.

I still have my conviction. These are last days. All should prepare their end, not seek it. Escape, abandonment, or rescue.

Here in the desert we can contemplate – the purity, the nothing – quite empty save for all the trash that traffic's left here, and the little compounds, scattered out along the line of sand and sky, like matchboxes, horizontal.

Waiting can last for ever, longer than us.

'Wait', says Bella, 'and be patient.'

'I'm ready. Thought of everything.'

I am the captain of the raft. I am in command.

And is this joy?

'Just wait!' Bella says. 'The sea will come to us.'

About the author

John Fraser has lived in Rome since 1980. Previously, he worked in England and Canada.